With a Name like Love

Tess Hilmo

SQUARE
FISH
Farrar Straus Giroux
New York

For David, who is Everlasting Love in so many ways

SQUARE FISH

An Imprint of Macmillan

Moody's song was written by the author.

Library of Congress Cataloging-in-Publication Data
Hilmo, Tess.
With a name like Love / Tess Hilmo.
p. cm.
Summary: Thirteen-year-old Olivene Love gets tangled up in a murder mystery
when her itinerant preaching family arrives in the small town of Binder,
Arkansas in 1957.
ISBN 978-1-250-02733-7
[1. Christian life—Fiction. 2. Conduct of life—Fiction. 3. Country life—
Arkansas—Fiction. 4. Arkansas—History—20th century—Fiction.
5. Mystery and detective stories.] I. Title.

PZ7.H566Wi 2011 [Fic]—dc22 2010036314

Originally published in the United States by Farrar Straus Giroux
First Square Fish Edition: July 2013
Book designed by Roberta Pressel
Square Fish logo designed by Filomena Tuosto
mackids.com

2 4 6 8 10 9 7 5 3 1

AR: 4.6 / LEXILE: 710L

With a
Name like
Love

Other books you may enjoy

1

It was the eighth of July, 1957, when Ollie's daddy slowed their rusted-out Chevy pickup near the junction of Highway 29 and Carter Road. They had come to set up for a three-day revival. Ollie sat in the truck bed with her sisters. She was thirteen and the oldest of Reverend Love's five daughters, followed by Martha, Gwen, Camille, and Ellen. Ellen was at Ollie's side, clutching Baby Doll Sue and singing "Mama's Little Baby." Ollie noticed her sister was getting the words twisted up and wrong—again.

It may have been only nine o'clock in the morning, but the summer sun was already high in the sky and sweating up the land. Fields of soft green barley laid themselves out across the earth in perfect rows—as if God had reached down and combed them just so. Ollie noticed a carved-up plank of wood that someone long ago had shoved into the dark Southern soil. It read: BINDER, ARKANSAS.

She closed her eyes and imagined what it might be like if her daddy drove past this small town and into the heart of a city. Maybe a preacher could make a decent living and buy a fixed-to-the-ground house with a mailbox, telephone, and refrigerator. Ollie thought it might even be a place where a girl could go to a real school and have an honest-to-goodness teacher, instead of being taught by her mother and a couple of hand-me-down books. It had to be worlds better than cramming into a 1941 travel trailer to sleep with the same four sisters every night. And oh—so much better than hitching up that trailer and disappearing down the road every three days. A city, Ollie imagined, was a place of possibilities.

Somewhere along the way, however, the good reverend decided a small town meant a poor town, and a poor town meant humble people. Ollie's daddy was born to preach to those people. His daddy had been a traveling preacher, as was his daddy before him, all the way back to the time of Moses. The Good Lord ushered him into that long line of preachers, and then his parents gave him the name Everlasting Love.

It was everything he was.

The truck rumbled to a stop at the edge of Carter Road. Ollie grabbed her satchel and jumped out of the truck bed. One of her jobs was to walk into town and spread word of their revival. She knew her daddy would turn around and head back to Mr. Marshall's place. That was the farmer who had agreed to let them use his spare field.

"Can I go, too, Mama?" Ellen hollered up to the front. "I wanna buy a new story for Baby Doll Sue with my chore dime."

"You're too young," Ollie said. She looked forward to those walks into town. It was about the only time she ever got to herself.

Susanna Love hung her head out the window. "Take your little sister," she said.

"But, Mama, they probably don't *have* a market. There's nothing for her to see."

"No back talk." Her mama's voice was snappy from the heat.

Ellen jumped out and gave her sister a told-you-so grin.

Ollie started walking.

Reverend Love waved goodbye and circled the Chevy back down Highway 29. Billows of dusty earth swirled out from the tires like smoke trailing off a campfire.

Ellen skipped over to Ollie and peered up at her with big, frog eyes. "You fixin' to get a soda?"

"Maybe I am and maybe I'm not."

"If'n you do get a soda, you fixin' to give me a sip?"

"There's likely no store, Ellen." Ollie reached over and pulled a stalk of rye grass that was growing tall. She stuck it in her mouth and chewed on the tangy end as the two girls continued up Carter Road and into town.

Ellen wasn't deterred. "I'm fixin' to get myself one of those new Golden Books with my dime, and I figure you might want to take a peek at my book. So it ain't rightful that you should look at my book if you don't share at least a tiny sip of your soda with me."

"*Isn't* right, Ellen. *Ain't* ain't a word."

"You get my meaning," the girl replied. "And don't think I'll forget you didn't give me a sip of your soda, 'cuz I won't."

"I haven't even gotten a soda yet! Who said I would? Maybe I'll get a book, too. Besides, we're supposed to be spreading these flyers." Ollie motioned to the white papers in her satchel. Well, mostly white. They were the same flyers they'd passed around the last few towns. Part of her job was shoving them into people's mailboxes or screen doors, and part was going back and picking them out of garbage cans before they left town, so they could be used again.

"Are you sayin' we ain't even gonna *look* for a market?" Tears immediately rimmed Ellen's bright eyes.

"We'll look."

"And you'll give me a sip?"

"*A* sip, Ellen. One."

"One is better than none," the girl said with new hope.

"Yes," said Ollie. "One is better than none."

• • •

Halfway into town, Ollie noticed a boy slinking along between the crowded poplar and ash trees that lined Carter Road. If he was trying to be sneaky about spying on them, he was doing a lousy job. Still, Ollie didn't mind. She was used to being other people's entertainment.

Ollie played along and pretended not to see the boy, with his orange shirt and scraggly brown hair. He continued to follow them, blending into the tree shadows, as they walked down the last bit of farm road and turned onto Main Street.

Binder was a pitiful place, worn thin from years of want. It was exactly like all the other towns her daddy dragged them through. It was exactly the kind of nothing Ollie had come to expect.

Except, maybe, for that boy.

Ollie walked casually along the tree-lined street until her curiosity got the best of her. She jumped into a thicket of poplars, where she thought she saw the boy hiding. "Gotcha!" she hollered.

No one was there.

"You heat crazy?" Ellen asked, Baby Doll Sue on her hip.

"No."

"Then whatcha screamin' at?"

Ollie took a long look behind the rows of trees and then scanned her eyes out across the fields. "Nothing," she finally said.

"Martha once told me about a girl who sat out in the sun all day and fried her brain," Ellen kept on, chattering a blue streak. "Fried it like eggs on a raddy-ator. Martha said the girl went so crazy her daddy sent her to a home for brain-fried people." Then Ellen stopped walking and tilted her head up to the heavens like a scrub jay. "Ollie, what's a raddy-ator?"

"Don't you know enough to ignore Martha?" Ollie shoved a flyer into a mailbox and sighed. Looking down Main Street, she could see a small spattering of buildings. There was a tiny schoolhouse, a store called Jake's Seed and Feed, an insurance office, a purple house called Knuttal's Quilting Cottage, a boarded-up Lutheran church, a sheriff's office, and a small clapboard building with a sign that read:

CARTER'S FRESH
GET IT HERE, OR DON'T GET IT

"They *do* have a market!" Ellen said. She bolted down the street toward the store.

A hard-looking woman met them out front. Ollie thought she looked like that famous picture from the Great Depression—the one her mama had shown her in an old magazine. It didn't take but a glance to know that, like the woman in the photograph, this woman had experienced more than a few difficult days in her life. She had two threadbare boys sitting at a card table off to the side of the market. They were flipping through a deck of cards at a furious pace. Slapjack. Ollie knew the game, though her daddy never allowed his girls to play with cards.

"Good morning. Is this your market?" Ollie asked, trying to sound friendly despite the wet heat streaming down the back of her neck and making her shoulder blades prickle.

"It is," the woman said. "Who's askin'?"

Ollie squared her shoulders and said, "I'm Olivene Love, oldest daughter of the Reverend Everlasting Love." Then she gestured to Ellen. "This here is my baby sister, Ellen."

The woman eyed the two girls with suspicion. "What's yer business?"

Ollie pulled a wrinkled flyer from her satchel. "Preaching, mostly—some singing and an occasional healing if the need arises." She handed the flyer to the woman. "The Marshalls have been kind enough to allow us to use their spare field. We welcome all to come see us at day's end."

The woman took the flyer and shoved it into her apron pocket. "How much did old Jeb charge ya?"

"Just the promise to leave the land clean as we found it." She knew her daddy offered Mr. Marshall the usual five percent of all collections, but figured that was their private family business.

The woman nodded, sucked in a wet breath, and shot a mouthful of brown spit onto the ground. Then she lifted the back of her hand and wiped tiny beads of tobacco juice off her chin. Ellen recoiled behind Ollie's skirt.

"That's tobacco," Ellen whispered, "and she's a *girl*."

"That ain't likely so," the woman said, replying to Ollie's statement. "Jeb Marshall ain't never done nothing without earning a profit in the matter."

Ellen slipped past the woman and into the dark market. Ollie shifted her feet and tried to think of a way to follow her baby sister. "Well," she said, "maybe it was my mama who talked to Mrs. Marshall. Women have a softer side toward strangers, you know."

"I know'd Eva Marshall since she was high as a tick's belly, and she ain't got a softer side toward no one."

"Everyone's got *some* goodness in them."

"Not everyone," the shop woman said, staring across the narrow street and into a small cluster of trees. "Some ain't even got a notion of goodness. Ain't that right, boys?"

The younger boy stopped his card in mid-air. "That's right, Mama," he said. "Some folks ain't born with any good a'tall." Then he flipped the card down and slapped the mound of cards centered on the table.

"Seems you'll be losing those, Joseph," the older

boy said, lifting his brother's hand from the pile. "That wasn't no jack. That was a queen."

Joseph slammed an angry fist into the corner of the rickety table, sending cards skittering to the ground.

Ollie looked to the shop woman, expecting her to chastise her son, but could see she was distracted by whatever she saw in the trees. Ollie let her eyes follow the woman's gaze. The dark green leaves on a poplar shivered and an orange T-shirt stood out from each side of the skinny trunk. Ollie walked over to the boy. "You spying on me?"

"Is it called spying if'n the person is walking about in public?" he asked, still hidden behind the tree.

"No, I suppose it's not."

"Then I'd say I'm not."

"Why don't you show yourself?"

It was quiet for the longest minute before the boy stepped out from his hiding spot. He was about Ollie's age, sorrily thin, and hadn't seen a speck of soap in weeks. Sweaty wisps of brown hair hung down over his warm, chocolate eyes.

Ollie took two cautious steps. She slid her hand into her satchel and pulled out another flyer. "You're welcome to come out to the preaching field tonight. My daddy's words are sure to chase away your sorrow," she promised. "And bring joy into your heart."

She pushed the flyer out toward the boy, but he didn't move. She bent down and laid the paper at his bare feet. "You'll be glad you came," she said. "Everyone is always glad once they hear my daddy sing his songs." Ollie paused and added, "Will you?"

The boy hesitated. "Maybe."

"And bring your folks?" Ollie knew, as much as Reverend Love enjoyed having children at his revivals, they usually didn't add much to the offering basket.

"Can't," the younger boy from Carter's said, coming up behind Ollie. "His pa's buried at the cemetery, and his sad excuse for a mama is jailed for the murder."

The boy took a step back into the tree shadows.

"Well then," Ollie said with a forced smile, "I'll save you a seat right next to me, up front where the listening is best of all."

The boy fixed his eyes on Ollie, saying nothing.

"I'll watch for you at sundown."

Still nothing.

Ollie walked back across the street and headed into the store. As she passed by, the shop woman muttered, "If'n you're asking me, I'd say you were looking for a mess of trouble invitin' that Koppel boy to your celebration. He'll bring bad luck upon you and your whole clan—plus shoo us *good* people away."

2

When the girls made it back to camp, it was Ollie's chore to flatten the rye grass and clumps of blue star in part of Mr. Marshall's field for the preaching canopy. Her daddy needed a smooth area to rest his podium, and folks needed a welcoming place to lay out their blankets. Ollie would also have to clear an area for their fire ring, table, and her parents' sleeping tent. As she worked, the words about that boy kept going through her mind—*sad excuse for a mama, murder, us good people.*

Ollie rested her chin on the rake and thought of the sorrow buried in that poor boy's eyes—sorrow too deep for someone so young.

"Keep to your chore," Reverend Love said as he walked by with his Bible open in his wide palm. Her daddy's hands were so big he could balance the thick book in just one. Ollie loved that Bible. It had belonged to her granddaddy, and her great-granddaddy before that.

"Daddy." Ollie dropped her rake and followed him. "Can I ask you a question?"

"Seems like you just did."

"Well," Ollie continued, "could there ever be a good reason for a wife to murder her husband?"

Reverend Love snapped his Bible shut and looked down into his oldest daughter's green eyes. "Is there a reason for this question?" He tried to hide the smile creeping up on his lips. "Has your mama been complaining?"

"Daddy!" Ollie laughed. "It's a boy I met today when we were passing out flyers. They say his ma killed his pa."

Reverend Love lifted his chin slowly and raised his eyebrows. "Is that what *they* say?"

Ollie knew what was coming.

"Be careful when you listen to people called *they*, Olivene," her daddy said. "*They* often tell lies."

He flipped his Bible open and walked away. She didn't follow him this time. She knew he needed to work on his recitation.

• • •

Once the large preaching canopy, yellowed from years of sun and rain, was arranged neatly in the middle of Mr. Marshall's field, the practicing began. Ollie and her sisters gathered around their daddy's preacher stand and rehearsed "Rock of Ages," "Abide with Me," and "This Little Light of Mine." Their daddy had taught them almost every gospel song ever written, but Ollie chose those three for their first night in Binder. It was another one of her responsibilities.

The evening would begin with the girls singing a welcome song while people got settled on their blankets. Reverend Love would then offer his sermon and invite his girls to sing a couple more songs. Once the air was buzzing with friendship and communion, the girls would step aside and allow their daddy to sing a song or two. He always sang last, waiting until the offering basket was being passed around. Reverend Love's voice was rich as molasses and deep as the Grand Canyon. It had a power about it that made people reach into their pockets even when they didn't come with the intention of donating to the cause. He called it his trademark. Ollie's mama called it their only salvation.

The sun dipped down along the horizon, casting long shadows across the field. Ollie and her family cleaned up from supper and made the final preparations for the revival. And as they did, they held their breath. Courting new patrons is like licking honey off a thorn—you have to go real slow and be extra gentle. They knew people wouldn't come out to the field if they felt like you were only there for the taking. And as much as Ollie disliked living out of their travel trailer, she knew her daddy was doing the best he knew how. It was the message—not the collections—that inspired their life.

"Let's turn some hearts tonight," Ollie's mama said. She said it at the start of every revival. Ollie watched her mama walk out to the edge of the field to wave in any worshippers. The early evening light settled around Susanna Love's shoulders, and streams of orange and scarlet danced in the sky above her head. Ollie noticed how her mama's long purple dress rippled around her thin legs in the breeze and couldn't help but marvel at how beautiful the whole scene was. It was like living poetry.

Her daddy always said he won the sweetest of all Georgia peaches when he took her mama's heart. He liked to tell his girls the story of how he met his wife when he was just a young man, starting out on the preaching road. One day, he saw her sitting in the back pew of a church in all her youthful glory. He walked directly up to her and said her smile was warmer than an August day in Savannah and would she please be his bride. Of course, she refused, but he kept after her. He'd sit outside the front window of her parents' house and sing old gospel songs deep into the night. In the end, it was his voice that wooed her.

"Sing out, girls," Ollie's mama hollered. "And don't look so glum—smile!" Ollie led her sisters in "Rock of Ages." "Can't you speed it up?" her mama called. "Folks don't need to hear a bunch of girls droning on. Put your heart into it!"

Martha, who was twelve, played the harmonica, while Ollie, Gwen, and Ellen sang out as loud as they could. Camille was simple in mind, so she always hummed along, holding Gwen's hand. Their music rose into the air, mingling with the soft chirps of crickets.

Ollie watched her mama bend over, pluck a single blue-star blossom and slip it into her amber curls. Ellen skipped out of formation and over to a bunch of the flowers. She plucked a handful of blossoms without any stems and shoved them behind her right ear. Ollie tried not to giggle as the loose flowers fell down onto the ground.

"Back in line," their mama said. Ellen returned to where her sisters stood, bottom lip pushed out in a pout. Susanna Love walked over, took the blossom from her own hair, and slid it into Ellen's. "There you go, baby girl," she said. "Pretty as a picture."

The people of Binder started to make their way out to the canopy. There were farmers wearing faded overalls and women in summer skirts. There were grandmas and grandpas, mamas and babies, daddies and sons—all gathered around to listen to Reverend Love's peaceful message and sing along with his powerful voice. All of them looking for something to ease the burden of their heavy lives. As Ollie sang, she thought it a familiar sight—just like every other revival, every other small town dotting the map from Kentucky down to Louisiana. Her family smiled and welcomed. They shook hands and learned names, but none of it meant anything. She knew they'd roll everything back into their trailer and move out when their three days were up. It would be no different here.

Once the welcome song was finished, and they were getting the last people settled, Ellen came over and slipped her hand into Ollie's. "Where'd all these folks come from?"

"Town, I suppose."

"But *where*?"

Ellen spoke the truth. There weren't that many homes in Binder, but patrons kept coming across the field, toward the canopy. From what Ollie could see, only one person was missing.

"I don't know, Ellen, but count it a blessing. Why don't you help Gwen pass out the Bibles?" Ollie stepped past the rows of blankets people had spread out on the flattened grass.

"Move over," she said to Martha and Camille when she reached the front of the crowd. The two girls sat on the yellow and pink patchwork quilt Ollie had spread out earlier, the one from Nana Shirlene, with green yarn ties on every square.

"You don't own this quilt," Martha said, stretching out diagonally. She was running a red pencil across the map book she always carried, drawing an *X* on the gray letters that said *Binder*.

Camille moved to the side.

"Don't move an inch, Camille," Martha said. "She's not the boss of us."

"I don't mind," Camille said.

Ollie didn't want to upset Camille. "Thank you," she said. Then she turned to Martha. "I'm saving a seat for someone. Could you please move?"

That got Martha's attention. "Who would you be saving a seat for?"

"None of your business."

"Fine," Martha said, turning back to her map book, but not budging. "Look, Camille. This shows there's a good-sized lake north of town. Wonder if there'll be any pike?"

"Martha," Ollie said.

Martha feigned great interest in her book. "Or even some trout."

"Fine." Ollie sat down and accidentally on purpose pushed her legs out, shoving Martha over to the side. Martha started to howl, but Reverend Love shot her a look that closed her mouth.

"Is this seat taken?" a shrill voice said from above. Ollie looked up to see the woman from Carter's Fresh standing over her. Her two boys stood at her side.

"I'm saving it," Ollie said.

"Oh right," the woman said, "for your new boyfriend." A wicked smile played on her lips.

"Boyfriend. Good one, Mama," the younger boy, Joseph, said. He shared his mama's dark eyes and apricot-colored hair.

"Come on, you two," the older boy said. "Leave her alone."

The woman tromped off, younger boy in tow, stepping on blankets as they went. The older boy gave Ollie an apologetic smile and followed his mama.

"Who was that?" Camille asked.

"Don't worry about it." Ollie wasn't in the mood to explain.

"Worry. Mental distress or agitation." Camille liked to read the dictionary and share her definitions. She was only eight and couldn't do lots of things, but she knew her Webster's and had been reading since she was five. "Can also mean to strangle or choke." She furrowed her brow.

"The first one," Ollie said, trying to dispel her sister's concern. "I'm just saying you don't have to think about it."

"That's right, Camille," Martha said. "Heaven forbid you have any opinions or ask questions."

Camille looked confused. Her limitations made it difficult to understand sarcasm. "Why not?" she asked.

"Oh never mind," Martha said.

Ollie turned her eyes out to the field, hoping the Koppel boy would show his face. All throughout the service, she kept looking for him. She had almost given up hope when she thought she heard some humming over by their Chevy. It was scratchy and out of tune, but it was a voice all the same. Ollie bent over, looking across the grass and under the truck.

Orange cotton poked out by the tire.

She quietly crept away from the quilt. "You made it," she whispered, trying not to distract from her daddy's preaching. "Why don't you come sit up front with me?"

He shook his head. "Them Carters are here. The older boy, Ralph, ain't so bad, but you gotta watch out for Joseph and their mama, Esther."

Ollie took him by the arm. "Don't worry. You're welcome here."

He jerked his arm away. "No such thing."

"Sure there is. Everyone's welcome in the preaching field."

A third voice came from behind Ollie. "Not everyone." She didn't have to look to know Esther Carter was standing behind her. "Go on, boy. Git."

The boy shoved his hands into his blue jeans pockets, turned, and sulked off toward town.

Ollie spun around and glared at Mrs. Carter. "What'd you do that for?"

"Certain towns have certain ways. Best you learn to abide by them."

Hot anger rushed up through Ollie's veins. "He's not some dog you can chase off."

Mrs. Carter turned back to the crowd. "You're right," she said over her shoulder. "A dog is good for something."

3

When the last bits of trash were cleaned up from the empty field and all of the spare Bibles were put back into their box, Reverend Love gathered the family around his knee. "We had a good night here in the field of God's simplicity," he said. "Ellen, you were a friend to all and I am mighty grateful."

"I got three address cards, Daddy," she said, her eyes all sparkles and joy. Collecting addresses from other children was Ellen's favorite part of their revivals.

"Camille," Reverend Love went on, "you brought the evening an air of grace and dignity only you can offer."

Camille blushed. "Dignity. The state of being honored, worthy, or esteemed."

"A perfect description," Reverend Love said. "Gwen?"

"Yes, Daddy?"

"You did a mighty fine job of sharing out the Bibles and making certain the little ones found the right passages."

Gwen beamed. "They're easy to find," she said. "If you know your Scripture."

Reverend Love nodded. "Martha, you keep getting better and better on that harmonica."

"It's not so difficult."

"And Ollie. What can I say about my Ollie? You set an example for your sisters in word and deed. I am blessed to call you mine. The songs you chose for tonight's service were perfect."

"Thank you, Daddy," Ollie said.

Reverend Love slapped his hands to his knees and said, "Time for bed. Surely, our next couple of nights here in Binder will be busy."

As they gathered around the wash bucket, the whole Love family stirred with excitement. All of them but Ollie, that is. She couldn't feel anything but sad.

Susanna Love directed her girls to sit on a felled log, from oldest down to youngest, and began braiding their hair for sleep. When the last strand of Ollie's chestnut hair was twisted and a red rubber band was fixed to the end, her daddy touched her gently on the shoulder.

"Care to say good night to the stars with me?" he asked.

"Of course," Ollie said. It was a rare privilege to be allowed to stay outside the trailer with the adults, and the offer nearly pushed aside her sadness. She followed her daddy under the broad summer moon as he cut through the tall, flowing grasses of the field. Ollie's daddy had a peacefulness about him that eased her troubled heart. It wasn't anything he did or said. It was just who he was, and how the wrinkles around his emerald eyes softened when he smiled at her. He was six foot five inches tall and thick as a slice of Grandma's bread. Ollie loved his dark wavy hair and bright green eyes. She thought her daddy could have been a movie star; he was that handsome.

"Good turnout tonight," her daddy said as he sat down on a patch of clover, leaned back on his elbows, and turned his face up toward the sleeping heavens.

Ollie sat down next to him. "It doesn't matter who comes if the person who needs it most isn't made to feel welcome."

Reverend Love nodded and let Ollie's words rest in the warm night air. Then he asked, "You stewing about that boy? The one whose mama you asked me about earlier?"

"Yes, sir."

"You feeling like he needed some kindness tonight?"

"Yes, sir."

Reverend Love let out a soft laugh. "Look at you," he said. "Already a shepherd, like your daddy."

"No," Ollie said. "That's not me. Gwen, maybe, but not me."

"Hmmm," her daddy said, deep in his throat. He reached over and pulled his daughter close. She snuggled into the crook of his arm and let the sharp, nutty smell of his Mennen deodorant soothe her troubled spirit. She thought of how incredibly lucky her mama was to have rights to his cuddle and smell every day of her life. Then, lying under the inky sky, Ollie's daddy began to sing. He sang quiet and soft. He sang the hymn she'd chosen as their welcome song that evening—"Rock of Ages"—because he knew it was her favorite. And as he sang, Ollie cried.

At first she cried about the Koppel boy and the sorrow that welled up in her when she remembered that forlorn look in his eyes. But after a while, she noticed how a whole army of other thoughts were slipping out of the crevices in her brain. It was like she opened a tiny window in her heart and every sad thought or pathetic situation in her history came slinking out. When Ollie was all cried out and her daddy was starting to doze off there in the field, she stood up. "Thank you, Daddy," she said. "I'm feeling much better."

Reverend Love rubbed his sleepy eyes, stood up, and took his daughter's hand. The two walked back to the trailer without a word. Right before he sent her to bed, Ollie's daddy said one last thing. "So, what are you going to do?"

He meant it more as encouragement than as a real question. Ollie nodded and ducked into the trailer. Her sisters were sleeping, so she felt her way through the darkness, changed into her nightgown, and slipped into bed. "Something," she finally whispered into the night. "Something."

4

Sun barely kissed the morning sky when Ollie jumped out of bed and began working her chores. She was praying she could talk her mama into letting her go into town and find that boy—the Koppel boy. Ollie knew they only had two more days in Binder and that boy needed a friend, if only for a short time.

The problem was that her family was somewhat famous for sleeping the morning away and seemed in no hurry to get this particular day moving.

First Ollie tried positive encouragement. She slapped bacon on the campfire and hoped the sweet, salty aroma would awaken them. She made a pot of strong coffee, with the wish that the dark ribbons of smell would tickle her mama's nose awake. Then she started on her chores, thinking that might do the trick. When none of it worked, Ollie began singing.

She didn't choose a soft gospel song like the one her daddy sang to her the night before. Instead, she chose a joyous, silly song and sang it out, loud as she could.

> "Oh my darling, oh my darling,
>   Oh my darling, Clementine!
>   Thou art lost and gone forever.
>   Dreadful sorry, Clementine."

She hadn't even finished the first verse when her mama stepped out of the tent she shared with Ollie's daddy.

"All right, Olivene, you've made your point. I'm up." Her mama wore a fuzzy blue bathrobe and white plastic slippers and had her hair flying out every which way. Even then, she was beautiful. "What's your hurry?"

"Just happy to do my work, Mama. I've started breakfast, sorted the trash from last night into burn piles, filled the wash bucket, and oiled all of the cast-iron pots."

"Since when have you been so anxious to work with the birds?"

"You're the one who always said the early bird gets the worm."

Her mama yawned and sat down on an overturned soapbox. "What's got you so antsy this morning?"

A rush of emotion pushed up into Ollie's heart, but she knew to be careful. Her parents likely wouldn't approve of her searching the countryside for an unknown boy with a murderous mama and an enemy in the Carter family. On the other hand, she had no intention of lying.

"I met a boy in town yesterday," she began.

"Your daddy said something about that."

"Well," Ollie continued, "I wanted to talk to him about daddy's service." It was all true, even if it wasn't the whole truth.

"And you think this boy will appreciate a caller so early in the day?"

"I'll be respectful," Ollie promised.

"I don't know," her mama said. "There's an awful lot of work to do around here."

"Please, Mama." Ollie put her whole soul into each letter of the word. "Please."

Susanna looked at her daughter and smiled. "All right then," she said. "Go on."

Ollie gave a tiny yelp of joy and started sprinting across the field.

"I expect you home no later than two o'clock,"

her mama called after her. "And you'll owe paybacks to your sisters for the chores they'll have to do for you today."

"Okay, Mama," Ollie yelled back, with a wave of her hand. "I promise."

Ollie skipped into town, feeling light and full of purpose. She had no idea what exactly she might say to that Koppel boy when she found him, but she hoped the Good Lord would guide her. After all, she was Olivene Love, daughter of the Reverend Everlasting Love. Words would surely come easy.

• • •

Like the first time Ollie walked into Binder, the plain brown clapboard of Carter's Fresh stood on the left. Mrs. Carter was nowhere to be seen, but Joseph sat on the steps striking matches on a blue matchbook and pinching the flame out with his bare fingers.

"Doesn't that hurt?" Ollie couldn't help but ask.

Joseph tilted his chin down and struck another match. Then he put the flame to his mouth and closed his lips around its orange heat.

"That's insane. You'll set your head on fire."

He offered a mischievous smile and pulled the doused match out of his lips. "You think *that's* insane?" he asked, as if it paled in comparison to all the other things he had done in his life.

"I don't think it's very smart."

"You callin' me dumb?"

Ollie eyed this boy. He couldn't have been more than fourteen but he was one of those boys who thought causing trouble would make him seem closer to sixteen or seventeen. Seeing him riled made her nervous. "No," she said. "I'm not calling you anything."

Holding a defiant glare, he pulled out another match, lit it, and stuck it in his mouth.

Ollie didn't want to waste any more of her day on the Carter family. "Suit yourself," she said, turning away from the steps and walking farther down the road.

"Always do," the boy called after her. "Always do."

She walked past the schoolhouse and the Lutheran church. She wondered why the church was abandoned and where people worshipped before her family came. She continued on to the sheriff's office, a red brick building with white shutters and chipped white steps. The front door was propped open with an electric fan, blowing high and loud. Ollie sucked in a deep breath and squared her shoulders. If she was going to find the Koppel boy, she figured this was a good place to start.

"Good morning," Ollie said as she stepped through the front door. It was dark inside, and she could only make out a window next to a bookcase and a row of chairs along the far wall. The earthy smell of stone tiles on the floor mingled with a heavy cloud of cigar smoke. Ollie could feel that smoke attaching itself to her dress, nestling deep into her curls.

"Morning to you," a deep voice called from within the musty darkness. "You lost?"

Ollie rubbed her fist to her eyes and stood still a moment while her vision adjusted to the darkened room. "No," she said. "I'm looking for the sheriff."

"S'at right?"

Now Ollie saw him. He sat below the window at a wide desk. He was a sickly looking man, with a long, thin face and a scraggly blond mustache. He wore a black felt cowboy hat and a denim shirt, and had a smoldering cigar shoved into the corner of his mouth.

"Yes, sir," she finally said.

"And what does a pretty lady like yourself need the services of a sheriff for?"

His words may have been flattering, but his manner gave Ollie the pure and undefiled willies. "You the sheriff?" she asked.

"I am. Sheriff Tommy Burton."

Ollie began to question her entire plan. She didn't trust Sheriff Burton. It may have been the way he was leaning back in his chair or the way he kept swirling that stubby cigar of his. She took a slow step back. "I . . . well, I . . . Never mind." Ollie quickly turned to leave and ran smack-dab into a lanky boy, likely around fifteen or sixteen. He was the spitting image of the sheriff—black cowboy hat, cigar smell, and all. He even had wisps of a blond mustache patched above his scrawny lip.

The boy grabbed Ollie by the shoulders. "Whoa there, where's the fire?"

"Let me go." Ollie tried to wriggle out of his grip.

"Settle down, I ain't gonna hurt you none."

Sheriff Burton stood up from behind his desk, walked over to Ollie, and gently took her by the arm. "I've got her, son," he said, flashing a tobacco-stained smile. "This here is my boy, Ray. Don't let him worry you none. He's training to be the next sheriff in line."

Ollie looked straight into the pale face of Sheriff Burton and asked, "Am I free to go now?"

He released his grip and raised his two hands in the air. "Suit yourself," he said. "You're the one who came knocking."

Ollie tugged on the waistline of her dress and smoothed out imaginary wrinkles in her skirt. "I apologize for taking your time." She took four steps out of the doorway and down the stairs.

"You lookin' for Jimmy Koppel?" Ray called out.

Ollie froze on the bottom step. *Jimmy.* So, that was his first name.

"Old Mrs. Carter said you were sweet on him, even asked him for a date."

"I invited him to my father's service," Ollie said. "Like I invited everyone else in town."

"That ain't what Mrs. Carter said."

"Well, she's telling you a lie. I just gave him a flyer." Ollie could feel her cheeks flush.

"And promised to save him a seat next to you?"

Ollie had promised to save Jimmy Koppel a seat, but only as an offering of friendship.

Sheriff Burton swirled the cigar in the corner of his mouth again and said, "I'd advise you to stay away from that boy. A sweet preacher's girl like yourself could only gain trouble from hanging around a Koppel." He pulled the cigar from his lips, stubbed it out on the oak railing leading into his office, and stuffed it into his back pocket. A lonely trail of smoke danced up from his mouth. "Does your daddy know you're scouring boyfriends out of Mason's Holler?"

"I am not!" Ollie said, louder than intended.

"Good," Sheriff Burton said. "Why don't we keep it that way?"

Ollie turned and stormed away. She didn't like Mrs. Carter before, but now she understood how evil that woman could be. Full-up bottled hatred, that's what Esther Carter sold in her store.

5

Ollie wandered farther down Main Street. She walked past Knuttal's Quilting Cottage, Jake's Seed and Feed, and Monson's Insurance, upset by Ray Burton's words. All the things she *should* have said and *could* have said began running across her mind. Awful as it was, though, she was glad she went to the sheriff's office. They had inadvertently given her both Jimmy's name and where he lived. Now she just needed to find Mason's Holler.

She passed a row of limestone houses and came upon a grandmotherly woman pruning a mess of pink roses in her front yard. Ollie recognized her from their revival the night before.

"Morning," Ollie called out.

The woman lifted a delicate hand to shade her eyes from the sun. "Oh, good morning," she said. "You one of the preacher's girls?"

"Yes, ma'am."

"How many of you are there anyway?" the old woman asked.

"Five." Ollie was used to the question.

"Five?"

"Yes, ma'am."

"Girls," the woman finished. "All girls."

Ollie expected judgment to seep into the woman's tone, but it didn't. Instead the woman mumbled something that sounded like *so blessed* as she resumed clipping the faded roses from the bush that twisted and wound itself around the white trellis on her front porch. Her yard brimmed and overflowed with rosebushes, lilac bushes, daylilies, crepe myrtles, and tall hollyhocks. Ollie thought it looked like a magnificent jumble of life—all pushing and fighting for a spot of sun and a sip of water.

"You have any?" Ollie asked, standing at the faded picket fence that lined the road.

"Any what, dear?" The woman didn't look up from her pruning.

"Girls," Ollie said.

The woman stopped her pruning shears and closed her eyes—for a moment, but long enough to let Ollie know she had crossed a line. Ollie started to apologize for her intrusion, but the woman answered first.

"Once," was all she said. Then she brought her smile back. "Is there something I can help you with, or are you just out walking on this beautiful summer morning?"

"I was wondering if you could tell me where I might find Mason's Holler."

The woman squinted her eyes real tight at Ollie and said, "Now, what would you need to know that for?"

"I'm looking for someone."

"Who, pray tell, are you looking for up Mason's Holler?"

Ollie held her breath a minute and then said, "Jimmy Koppel."

The woman gave a slow shake of her head and walked over to the fence where Ollie stood. "You seem to be a good girl," she began.

Ollie's gut twisted.

"I knew it from the moment I laid eyes on your godly family," the woman continued. "Your pa is the salt of the earth."

Ollie steadied her feet that were itching to walk away.

"So," the woman went on, "it is because I regard

you highly that I say these things. Mason's Holler is not for you. Best you mind your business over in these parts."

Ollie thought how her daddy once said sometimes people do things out of ignorance more than meanness. That's what Ollie took this woman to be—ignorant of God's love more than mean-spirited toward others.

"Can I ask you a question then?" Ollie said.

"I suppose."

"Did Jimmy Koppel's mama murder his daddy?"

The old woman tick, tick, ticked her tongue like a clock. "Well, I see you've gotten yourself all tied up in a mess of curiosity. You know what they say about the cat, don't you?"

"But did she?"

The woman gave two more clicks of her tongue. "Word is she confessed and signed it to paper."

"But why?" Ollie pressed.

"*Why not* would be a better question. Henry Koppel never brought anything but misery to that poor woman. No, not many of us are asking why she did it—more like, how come it took her so long?"

Now Ollie better understood what she saw in Jimmy Koppel's eyes. It wasn't the murdering, but everything that might have led his mama to the terrible point of murder. More than ever, she wanted to talk to him. "Mason's Holler?" she asked again with hope in her heart.

"Jimmy's a good boy. Still, I worry about you getting mixed into all of that unrest."

Ollie offered up her pleading face.

"All right," the woman said, nodding at a dirt path north of the main road.

"Thank you," Ollie said. "Thank you, Mrs. . . ."

"Mahoney," the woman answered.

"Thank you, Mrs. Mahoney." Ollie took off toward Mason's Holler. She wandered up the rocky path that twisted between two hills. The blue sky covered her head, and stocky pines shaded her feet. The air was a bit cooler and carried a feel so very different from the farming patches laid out below the holler. She hadn't traveled more than fifteen minutes, but felt miles away from every care.

At first, she didn't see many signs of life—a can of Swenson's cling peaches, swollen from the heat and left by the roadside, a single brown tennis shoe hanging from the branch of a mulberry tree, a rusted-out wagon handle.

As Ollie continued along the path, though, she heard a deep and soulful tune. Someone was singing with a voice like her daddy's. She walked until the holler's walls opened up into a patchy field. One home sat in the middle. It was a tired old place—likely held together with chewing gum and spit—but Ollie noticed its dirt yard was swept in long, even rows and purple impatiens dotted two neat flower-boxes on the front porch. She held back behind a sturdy pine and took in the sight. The voice she heard was coming from a colored man, sitting on his front porch and whittling a trinket box. Ollie didn't recognize the song he was singing, but knew it had to be back from the beginning of time.

> "So alone, forlorn and aching,
>   Reaching for the reverent light.
>   Reach on out, God's love will save you.
>   Save your soul, lead you aright."

The smoky notes filled the morning air, and his voice, smooth as glass, rolled the sweet words off his tongue and right into Ollie's heart.

> "For He knows cold, and He knows hunger.
>   He knows pain no man can bear.
>   Let His light shine in and lead you.
>   Lead you on, lead you home."

"That's a beautiful song," Ollie said, taking courage to step out of the shadows.

The man looked up from his handiwork, and then back down. "Not nice to jump up on an old man like that," he said. "Likely send me to an early grave."

Ollie thought it wouldn't have been *too* early, judging by his crumpled skin and the wiry gray hairs twisting out of his ears and nose.

"Sorry," she said.

"No mind," the man replied, keeping his head down to his work.

Ollie walked over to the porch. "Hello," she said. "I'm Olivene Love, oldest daughter of the Reverend Everlasting Love."

The man raised his eyebrows and tipped his head to the side. "You say that a lot?"

"Yes, sir."

"Thought so."

Ollie sat down next to him on the steps.

He chewed on his bottom lip and peered into Ollie's face. "You got business with me?"

"No, sir. I'm looking for Jimmy Koppel."

"Is that so?" He turned back to his whittling.

"Yes, sir. What's the name of that song you were

singing?" Ollie asked. "My daddy knows just about every song ever writ, but I never heard that one."

"No name."

"How can that be? Every song has a name."

"Can't have a name if you never gave it one."

Ollie couldn't hide her surprise. "You wrote that song?" She could see that the man felt uncomfortable with her questions, but she couldn't help herself. "You write any other songs?"

"Some."

"Will you sing one for me?"

"Didn't know I stepped onstage."

"Well, will you at least come out to the preaching field tonight and sing that last song for my daddy? We're down by the Marshalls' place."

The old man kept to his work. He was carving the tiny box with intricate roses and diamonds cascading down the side. Ollie thought it was one of the most beautiful things she had ever seen—especially the tiny gold clasp that fixed the lid shut.

"Does that daddy of yours know where his daughter is?" he said, not looking up.

"Well enough. He knows I'm looking for Jimmy Koppel, and he knows I can mind my way around a new town. So, will you come to the canopy tonight, Mr. . . ."

"Moody."

Ollie stretched out her hand. "Pleasure to meet you, Mr. Moody."

"No mister. Just Moody." He laid down his whittling knife, wrapped his warm, tissue-paper hand around Ollie's, and gave a gentle squeeze. "And I prefer to keep my singin' to my front porch." She could feel the warmth of his friendship pouring down from his heart, through his arm, and right out of his fingertips. It was pure liquid. It was divine.

6

Moody didn't ask Ollie why she wanted to go to the Koppel place. Unlike Sheriff Burton, he didn't warn her against the horrible things that would happen to her precious soul if she befriended the boy. Unlike Mrs. Mahoney, he didn't assume she'd be over her head in trouble. He just pointed out the way and let her go. And as Ollie walked away, she said a prayer that Moody would change his mind and take her up on the invitation to join them for services that night. She was certain her daddy would enjoy that sorrowful, hopeful tune of his.

Ollie walked farther into the holler. Air in Arkansas is thick in the summertime. That's good for the gnats—they float around by the thousands on invisible streams of heat—but it's not so great for people. The sun was centered in the sky and all traces of morning coolness had burned away. Ollie shone with the day's humidity, and her chestnut hair frizzed from the ends out. She pulled her fingers through her natural curls, her mother's curls, and tried to smooth them with the wetness sopped up from her brow. For as beautiful as it was there in Mason's Holler, it was hotter than Hades.

"Lordy, Lordy," Ollie mumbled to herself as she fiddled with her curls.

"Ain't it like the preacher's child to be the one swearing."

Ollie spun around and saw Jimmy Koppel standing next to a bellflower tree.

"I didn't swear," she said, "and besides, what are you doing sneaking around on me?"

"Don't you know your commandments?" He was half laughing, half accusing, and Ollie didn't like any of it. She started getting riled, but then caught a glimmer in Jimmy's eyes that made her soften. She couldn't place it, but something about the sight of him sent a warm rush right through to her toes. He wasn't exactly what she might call good-looking, although she couldn't tell what he might truly look like if he scraped the layers of grime off his skin. The same orange T-shirt from the day before hung loosely from his bony shoulders, and his face was altogether too sharp to be considered handsome. Mostly, it was his eyes that got her.

Ollie reached her hand out. "I never introduced myself properly. I'm Olivene Love, oldest daughter of the Reverend Everlasting Love. You can call me Ollie."

"All right."

"Well," Ollie said, dropping her hand. "Aren't you going to introduce yourself?"

"Why?" Jimmy asked. "When it's plain you know who I am."

"Still," Ollie said, "when a lady extends a hand . . ."

"If you're callin' *twelve* a lady."

"Thirteen and two months."

Jimmy didn't look impressed. "If you say so."

"I do," Ollie said. "Besides, I'm just trying to be friendly. You got something against friends?"

"No," he said. "And for the record, I wasn't sneakin' around on you. I'm out huntin' frogs."

Ollie hadn't noticed the sawed-off milk carton at his feet. It was twitching all on its own. "You keep 'em in there?" she asked.

"Yep."

"Can I see?"

"No mind."

She stepped over and peered down into the carton. Three tiny globs of gray frogs clambered up the side and slid helplessly back down on top of one another. Jimmy reached one hand in and scooped up a single frog. He cupped his other hand over the first and held it out to Ollie. When she tilted her head and looked between Jimmy's thumbs, she could see the watery black eyes of the frog staring out at her.

"What do you do with them?" she asked.

"Keep 'em, mostly. But some aren't good for keeping. Like the bird-voiced tree frog. They got a slime that'll burn your eyes. If I come across one of them, I look from a distance."

Jimmy told her all about the frogs he collected. Ollie thought he might know more about frogs than her daddy knew about the Holy Bible. He told her about the pickerel frog, and how its sweat was a poison that killed anything you put in the same carton with it—including other frogs. He told her about the crawfish frog, and how it would eat other frogs. The more Jimmy talked about frogs, the more Ollie began to dislike the creatures. She tried to hide the look of disgust creeping up on her face, but he saw it all the same.

"There are good frogs, too," he said defensively

and in a clear effort to redeem the en
"These here are sweet gray tree frogs. T
much of anything. They don't even screa
pick them up."

"Frogs scream?"

"Sure. You'd call it a croak, but if you knew them better then you'd know it sounded different from a regular croak . . . higher. That's a scream."

Jimmy told Ollie how he had been gathering frogs since he was only four years old, and how he had a whole frog ranch up the road at his house.

"I've never seen a frog ranch," Ollie said. "Will you take me?"

Jimmy's face darkened. "You don't want that."

"I'll be the judge of how to spend my day, thank you very much, Jimmy-the-frog-boy Koppel." She meant it as a tease, so it surprised her when he took it as a grand compliment.

"I do know a bit about frogs."

"Are you kidding me?" Ollie said. "You're a full-blown expert. What's a frog expert called anyway?"

"A herpetologist."

"Right," Ollie agreed, as if she had a clue. "A herpetologist, that's what you are. Though I can't definitively say until I see your display of knowledge—until I see the ranch."

Jimmy put the frog back into the carton and started walking deeper into the holler. "Course," he continued, "nighttime's best for frog huntin', or early morning, since most frogs are nocturnal. Unless'n a storm passes through. That'll bring 'em out by the hundreds." Jimmy shook his head and laughed. "Though I guess that's only right. You'd climb out of your bed, too, if it was gettin' flooded out by a rain-storm." Then Jimmy stopped walking and turned back to Ollie. "You know what *nocturnal* means?"

"Yes, I know what *nocturnal* means."

"Just checkin'. I got these guys as they headed back into the marsh for some shut-eye." He nodded down at the cardboard milk box in his hand.

"Lucky you," Ollie said.

"I'd say! Another ten minutes and they'd be impossible to find."

7

Ollie couldn't help but wonder what God might think when He looked down upon Mason's Holler and saw the shack Jimmy Koppel called home. Up to that minute in her life, Ollie had honestly believed *any* home would be better than the travel trailer her daddy pulled around on the hitch of his Chevy. But standing there looking at the Koppel place, she rethought the matter completely.

Where there was ground, there was trash, and a rotten stench rose up from every direction. The house itself—or what bits of it were left—tilted sharply to the right as if it would fall over with the slightest breeze. Scraps of quilting fabric hung in the tiny window openings at either side of the front door. Ollie noticed Jimmy watching her face carefully, maybe looking for signs of disappointment. She was determined not to give him any.

"Mama always kept better care," he said. "I would have cleaned if I knew I was gonna have company."

"How long has your mama been away?" she asked.

"Two weeks."

There was no way the Koppel place was anywhere near clean two weeks before, but Ollie tried not to mind. It wasn't her worry how Jimmy's mama kept house. She guessed it was the least of his worries as well.

"Do you miss her?" Ollie kept her gaze to the horizon.

"I suppose. Nights mostly."

"Who's taking care of you?"

"I can manage on my own," Jimmy said. "There's plenty of fish in the creek, and I have a friend down the road who helps me out a bit."

"Moody?"

Jimmy smiled. "So you met him."

"He's got some voice," Ollie said.

"Moody's been good to us. I'll be sad when the bus comes to take Mama to Little Rock and Sheriff Burton makes me leave here." He looked out across the rows of milk cartons.

"Where will you go?"

Jimmy shrugged. "They say I have an aunt in

Tennessee. My daddy's sister. I didn't even know she existed, but Sheriff Burton did some digging and sent her a letter telling her she has a legal responsibility to take me whether she wants to or not. I'll be heading there once my mama is sent to the state prison in Little Rock."

"Why wouldn't she want you?"

Jimmy looked at Ollie. "If she hated my daddy, she might not be thrilled to have his son come knocking on her door."

"I'm sure she didn't hate him."

"Everyone hated him," Jimmy said. He took a slow breath. "Hey, do you want to see them frogs or not?"

"Absolutely."

He led her over to the side patch of yard, where row after row of sawed-off Pure Pak cardboard milk cartons lined the field. There was not a speck of trash in this area—just twenty or more immaculate rows of the boxy white cartons. Not one was out of alignment. It was a perfect orchard of friends.

Four large tarps hung between tall pines, shading the milk cartons from the hot sun, and buckets of water were lined up along the front. Ollie noticed how each carton had a square of net draped over the opening.

"Where did you get all these milk cartons?"

"Sometimes I dig 'em out of people's trash. You'd be surprised what you can find if you've got an eye for it. Other times I'd wake up to a few sittin' there on my porch, along with some cans of beans or piles of scrap fabric. It was real nice, but it stopped after Mama left."

"Do you know who left those things?"

Jimmy shrugged. "I didn't see anyone, and they never wrote a note. I thought you came to see the frogs."

"I did," Ollie said.

"All right then, let's get to it." He walked over to the first row of cartons. "I keep the green trees over here by the oaks, and pickerels are lined up by themselves on the east side. Cope's frogs like the morning sun, so they need to be on the most western side to catch the rising sun. That's common sense."

"Of course it is," Ollie said with a nod.

"These here are the pickerels," he said as he walked over to the eastern line of milk cartons. "Some get 'em mixed up with the leopard frogs, but I know the difference." Jimmy lifted up a carton and tilted it toward Ollie. She peered in and saw a fat brown and yellow spotted frog. "See that orangey section there on his hind legs?"

"Yeah," Ollie said, leaning in.

"That's what makes him a pickerel. Leopard frogs have the same spots and colors, but don't have this orange tone to their legs." Jimmy was practically glowing.

"That's amazing."

Jimmy reeled off list after list of facts on each frog, and then he would hesitate, looking over at Ollie to gauge her reactions. She couldn't help but feel as if he didn't trust her interest, so she kept trying to reassure him by saying things like "That's fantastic" and "How in the world did you ever learn that?" She drew on her mama's talent of finding the good in any situation and complimented Jimmy on his organization system and the clever way he kept just the right amount of water in each jug. He told her where he hunted for beetles, crickets, and silkworms to keep them all fed.

"Do you hunt frogs every day?" Ollie asked.

"Most days, but I don't always take what I find. I'd be swarming in 'em if I brought 'em all home."

Ollie looked out across Jimmy's ranch. That boy must have had nearly a hundred frogs in tidy rows, and she wondered if he wasn't swarming in them already.

"Do you ever let them go?" she asked.

"Sure. I get 'em and keep 'em and then tie one of these strings around its hind legs before I set it free." Jimmy reached into his jeans pocket and pulled out a roll of cream-colored string. "You gotta be sure to tie it just right and keep the ends short. I wouldn't want the string to cause 'em any trouble."

"Quite important," Ollie said.

"It's my system for not catching the same frog twice."

"And you can say hello when you run into it again," Ollie said with a smile.

"Exactly."

Ollie noticed a small cluster of cartons nestled beneath some scrub oak that Jimmy hadn't said a word about. "What's with these over here?" she asked, walking over to the grouping.

"Wait," Jimmy began, but it was too late. Ollie was already peering down into the cartons. In the bottom of each was a damaged frog—some with one leg ripped off, some with two or three. A couple of the frogs had black circles burned into their backs, and one looked like someone had scratched out its eyes. Ollie slowly pulled back from the frogs.

"Who would do such a thing?" she said.

"My pa," Jimmy answered. The words were like hundred-pound weights dropping out of the air.

Jimmy joined Ollie by the damaged frogs and knelt down. He reached into one carton and gently cradled a two-legged frog in the soft belly of his palm.

"He'd say," Jimmy began—although he seemed to be talking to the frog more than to Ollie—"'You didn't do your work right, son. Fetch me a frog.' Or sometimes, when he got to drinking too much, he'd grab one himself. These he pulled the legs from, but these over here"—Jimmy pointed to the ones with the black circles on their backs—"he took his cigarette to. Most died. I only managed to save a few."

Ollie sat down. "That's terrible," she said. "But honestly, Jimmy, wouldn't they be better off if you let them die?"

Jimmy looked sharply at Ollie. He steeled his eyes, and she noticed his jaw clamp tight and begin to twitch. "No," he said. "Even a broken life is better than no life at all. At least they get to see the sunrise and taste a cool drink in the afternoon heat. That's something."

Ollie was sorry she'd said anything. In fact, she was sorry she ever saw the damaged frogs. It brought a sorrow to Jimmy he couldn't seem to shake. He sat there on the ground and pulled the cartons of hurt frogs all around him. He lifted each frog out of its carton, one at a time, and whispered kind words to it. "You'll be all right," he said. "You're a strong little guy."

Ollie scooted closer to her new friend. She didn't say a word and kept her eyes out to the field, watching white tufts from the cottonwood trees float around on the hot breeze.

After a long time of sitting quietly, with Jimmy tending and loving those beat-up frogs, Ollie said in a soft voice, "Now I understand. Now I see how she could do it."

Jimmy looked up. "But that's just it, Ollie. My mama didn't do it. She had every right to, we all did. Still, she didn't do it."

And Ollie knew to the core that Jimmy was telling her the truth.

8

Everyone in her family was busy working when Ollie returned to the preaching field.

"You're late," her mama hollered out from behind a sheet she was pinning to the line.

"Only a few minutes."

"It's three o'clock. Since when is an hour a few minutes? I was starting to worry about you."

Ollie scurried over and began helping her mama pin up the laundry. "Sorry," she said. "It was important."

"Well," her mama said, softening, "I suppose it's all right. But let's not make this a habit."

"I promise, Mama."

"And you owe a thank-you to your sisters, especially Martha and Gwen. They've carried your load today."

"Yes, ma'am."

"And after you've finished your work and thanked your sisters, your daddy wants to see you."

"Yes, ma'am."

Ollie's mama turned over the laundry to her and began stoking the fire for supper. Ollie pulled Ellen's yellow and white polka-dotted dress out of the basket and hung it on the line. Then she pulled out a pair of her own bloomers. Ollie purely hated hanging her bloomers on a line for the world to see. It was another reason she longed for a real house—water and electricity. She didn't understand why her mama wouldn't insist on having a home so she could use a washing machine and dryer. Wouldn't any red-blooded American woman want that?

Ollie thought back to when they set up a revival in Martin, Georgia, about ten stops back. That town had an amazing place called Magic Suds Laundr-O-Mat, and after some begging, Reverend Love allowed his girls to go in and utilize the electric washers and dryers.

Ollie remembered her mama tossing a whole pile of dirty clothes into the washing machine, pushing their coins into the slot, and then standing back and watching the magic happen. Ellen sat on top of the dryers and crooned about how warm her legs felt. Ollie, Martha, Gwen, and Camille played jacks while the power of electricity did all of their work. It was a beautiful day for the Love sisters. Ollie sighed at the sweet memory and hung her bloomers on the same pins as Ellen's dress, with the bloomers facing the back field. It was a trick she used for privacy.

Ellen came up from behind the laundry, pushing her face and spread-eagled arms into a white sheet. "Oooooo," she moaned like a ghost. "Ooooooo."

"Oh no," Ollie said in a flat tone, "a ghost. I'm *so* scared."

Ellen stepped out from behind the sheet with her fists planted firmly on her hips and said, "You sure know how to climb on a girl's last nerve."

Ollie rolled her eyes as Ellen stomped back to the travel trailer, where Martha was sitting on their brown stool, mending the hem on Mama's blue calico skirt.

"Never mind her, Ellen," Martha said, not looking up from her sewing. "She's too busy traipsing all over creation to play with her own baby sister."

"I'm not a baby," Ellen whined.

"That's right," Ollie said. "She's not. Besides, I was doing something important."

Martha looked up and raised a single eyebrow—it was a special talent of hers. "Right."

"I was," Ollie said. "And I had permission, so it's none of your business."

"Meanwhile, I had to cart the water all the way over from Mr. Marshall's spigot and do the baking," Martha said. "By myself."

"Not true," Ellen said. "Camille pounded the biscuits. I saw her."

Martha wasn't deterred. "And since I was doing your share of the work, I never got any time to explore the lake I saw on my map. We might've had fresh trout or pike for dinner tonight, but I guess our empty bellies aren't important to you."

Ollie pinned the last dress to the line and lifted the basket back to its resting place by the travel trailer. "Thank you, Martha," she said. "I owe you."

"You can start by finishing the mending." Martha pushed the skirt into Ollie's hands. "It's *my* turn for a walk."

"Can I come, too?" Ellen pleaded. "Can I, huh? Can I?"

Their mama hollered from the campfire, "No one is going anywhere. There's too much to do before the service tonight." She was shoving the iron poker into the roots of the fire and shielding her eyes from the flying sparks. "Olivene, have you spoken to your father yet?"

"No, ma'am."

"Well, get to it."

"Yes, ma'am."

Ollie handed the mending back to her sister. Martha stuck out her tongue. Ollie gave her a satisfied grin.

"I can see you," their mother said.

"Sorry," both girls said in unison.

Neither meant it.

• • •

The parents' tent was behind the travel trailer, right next to their portable outhouse tent and faithful truck. There was a time when the entire Love family slept in the trailer together, but that was before Camille and Ellen came along. Now Everlasting and Susanna slept separate from their girls in an army green double-flap.

Ollie stepped inside the tent and quietly waited to be acknowledged. Her daddy was sitting on the edge of his cot, Bible open across his lap, tablet of paper and pencil in his hands. Ollie thought he must have been working on something particularly inspiring because he was scribbling notes and nodding.

After a long minute, Reverend Love let his pencil come to rest and turned to his oldest girl. "How'd it go?" he asked.

"Good," Ollie said. "I found him."

"And?"

Ollie sat down on her mama's cot, next to her daddy, and fiddled with her thumbs on her lap. She wasn't certain how much she should tell him.

"His name is Jimmy Koppel," she decided to say.

"That's a fine name," her daddy said. He was good that way. He never pushed for information the girls weren't ready to give. "I look forward to meeting him."

Her daddy turned back to his notes, which let Ollie know the conversation was over. She wanted to tell her daddy how Jimmy's mama was in jail for a murder she didn't commit, and how she never even had a legal trial, but Ollie knew she must wait. Right before her daddy gave a sermon was never a good time to talk about personal matters. He was too focused on his work.

So Ollie decided to bide her time and hope for a good turnout at that night's revival. If the collection basket was full, and if her daddy felt like he was making a difference in a life or two, he would be in better spirits to hear what Ollie needed to say—how the family had to stay in Binder longer than three days. How they needed to stay as long as it took to solve the murder of Jimmy's daddy.

9

Once the afternoon chores were finished and the family had their supper, it was time to get ready for services. Ollie stepped inside the travel trailer as her mama was fixing the last button on her lime green skirt. She watched her mama sit down on a chair and twist her long amber hair into a loose bun, tendrils falling softly around her face.

"Get yourself ready," her mama said, not looking away from the oval mirror that was perched on the table in the corner.

Ollie slipped into a fresh blouse and slowly worked the buttons as she secretly watched her mama finish dressing. Susanna smoothed her long legs into white stockings and pushed beige shoes with square heels onto her delicate feet. That woman was a sight to be seen.

"Mama?" Ollie asked, not at all knowing where

the words were coming from. "I found him. The boy."

"Did you?"

"Yes. And I met the sheriff and his son and a lady named Mrs. Mahoney and a man named Moody— boy, can he sing! He was singing the most magical song, and he even said—"

"Olivene Love, we do not have time to relive your day. Now I'm glad you had an opportunity to make a few friends. Lord knows you need some in your life."

"It's more than that, Mama. There's something not right in this town."

Susanna turned and looked at Ollie. "Whatever are you talking about?"

"Something's wrong."

"Now, child, don't let your imagination run wild. There is nothing in this town that hope and prayer can't lift."

Ollie was pleading with her mama. "It's more than that. Some of the people here are acting terrible to this boy."

Ollie's mama was not amused. "Who?" She turned back to the mirror, twisted up a tube of pink lipstick, and gently pressed the color to her mouth.

"Mrs. Carter, for one. And her hooligan sons. Maybe Sheriff Burton and his son as well."

"Now you listen to me and you listen well, do you hear?"

"Yes, ma'am."

"First off, we don't go around calling God's children hooligans. Second off, you can't know a person in one day. Don't be so quick to judge others." Susanna sat down next to Ollie and pulled her in close. She had a way of being tender with her girls when the moment called for it. "You'll see. Everything will be fine." She kissed Ollie on the forehead and said, "Have you picked the songs for tonight?"

"What's the sermon?" Ollie asked, wiping away the lipstick mark her mama had left on her forehead.

"Pride, I believe."

Ollie thought that was a perfect topic. If the people of Binder truly understood no one person was above another, they might not be so awful to Jimmy just because he happened to be born to a no-good father. A child, she knew, has no choice where God will send it.

She immediately decided the welcome hymn should be "Amazing Grace." She also decided that, if they came, she'd seek out the faces of Esther Carter and that weasel Ray Burton on the line "that saved a wretch like me" and give them a nod. They were wretched.

Ollie called her sisters together for practice. Martha and Ellen were pulling the laundry off the line. Camille sat quietly by the fire. Gwen, on the other hand, had to be searched out of the far field. She was out there studying her Bible. Gwen was the most like her daddy, with dark hair and fresh white skin. She was born with a hankering for preaching, too, and would have made an excellent preacher—if only she were a boy. Ollie knew her daddy was certain another preacher boy was itching to come down into his family line, but she also knew her mama had a different opinion.

The girls readied the Bibles and calmed the fire. They dusted off the preaching stand and tightened the tent ropes and set out clean trash containers. All the while, Ollie thought about Jimmy and his ripped-up frogs. It saddened her to no end, but for the first time she felt like she had purpose. Like maybe God Himself was saying to her, "Olivene Love, you've been praying to me for thirteen long years. Well, I'm finally listening. I'm gonna give you that friend. It's a messy thing, and you might have to figure out a problem or two, but if anyone can do this, I believe you can."

Ollie nodded. "All right, Lord," she said under her breath. "I sure hope you are right."

• • •

Not as many townsfolk came out to the preaching tent that evening. Of course, the Love family didn't expect the same turnout they enjoyed on their initial night in Binder. They knew curiosity will bring most everyone out to the field on the first night, and fewer and fewer on each subsequent night. That is why they kept to their three-night rule. It was the nature of the work. Even so, it was unusual to go from an overflowing field one night to a half-empty field the next. Ollie thought back on her trip into town and wondered if her nosing around had cost her family.

One of the people who did come was Mrs. Mahoney. She searched out Susanna and complimented her on raising such fine girls, commenting on her meeting with Ollie earlier that day. Then she found her way over to Nana Shirlene's quilt, sat down, and slid Ellen up onto her lap.

Like a born grandmother.

"You girls are so smart," Ollie heard her tell Ellen and Camille, "I'll bet you like riddles."

Ellen bounced and bubbled on the old woman's lap. "I'm 'specially good at riddles," she said.

"Well, that's very lucky," Mrs. Mahoney said, wrapping her arms around Ellen and giving her a calming cuddle. "I happen to have one that's perfect for girls who are *'specially good at riddles.*"

"That's me," Ellen said. "And Camille," she decided to concede.

Mrs. Mahoney added, "And I have a peppermint for whoever gets the answer."

Ellen was all ears.

"Listen well," Mrs. Mahoney began.

> "Little Nanny Etticoat
> In a white petticoat,
> And a red nose;
> The longer she stands,
> The shorter she grows."

Ellen scrunched up her face and flicked a finger at her temple. "Say it again," she said.

Mrs. Mahoney repeated the riddle, slow and steady. She looked to Camille, who was wearing a proud smile. "Do you know the answer?"

Camille leaned over and whispered something into Mrs. Mahoney's ear.

"Excellent! I knew you were a clever girl." She reached into her apron and pulled out a red and white peppermint.

"Not fair!" Ellen whined. "Camille's brain works in riddles. It's easier for her."

Mrs. Mahoney asked Camille, "Shall we tell her?"

Camille nodded and said, "A candle."

Ellen shook her head, rethinking the riddle. "Is her red nose the flame?"

"See?" Mrs. Mahoney said. "You are clever, too." She handed Ellen a candy, then turned and gave one to Gwen, Martha, and Ollie, who sat off to the side.

Just then, Reverend Love stepped up to his podium and started the service. Every minute Ollie wasn't required to be up front singing or passing the collection basket, she snuck out toward the welcome path, searching for a speck of orange between the trees in the far thicket or behind the Chevy.

She never saw one.

She kept asking herself why her concern about Jimmy should matter, but knew it did. Binder was no different from every other small town in the South. They had their own way of doing things and didn't appreciate outsiders coming in and causing problems. And even though the collection basket wasn't nearly as full as the night before, Ollie knew she needed to speak to her daddy about helping Jimmy and his mama.

10

After everyone had left and the field had been cleaned up, Ollie sat down with her daddy. She told him what Jimmy had said about his mama's innocence, about the torn-up frogs Jimmy tended, and about the way the boy was pretty much alone in his troubles. Nothing spoke to Reverend Love like a neglected soul.

He agreed to consider her request to stay longer, with the condition she take ~~him~~ directly to Jimmy the next day.

"It's not fair," Ellen whined when morning came and she saw Ollie getting ready. "How come I can't go?"

"Because I need you here," her mama said as she scraped another batch of burned eggs from their cast-iron skillet. Eggs were nearly impossible to cook over an open fire, even for Susanna Love.

"Ollie gets everything good," Ellen kept on, "and I never get nothin'!"

"*Anything*," her mama corrected. "You never get *anything*."

"I know!"

Gwen tried to help. "But, Ellen," she said, "if you go with Ollie, you'll miss out on the dandelion necklaces I was going to teach you how to make today."

"The ones with the yellow flowers?" Ellen wiped tears from her ruddy cheeks.

"The very ones," Gwen promised. "I'll teach you and Camille, both."

"Dandelions," Camille said. Then her face fell blank. "Dandelions," she tried again. She flipped her pocket Webster's out and began pushing through the pages. Funny, Ollie thought, which words she knew and which she didn't. It didn't seem to upset her any—not knowing the definitions. It just gave her something to do.

"You might as well get used to it, Ellen," Martha said, ignoring Camille. "Ollie gets everything good."

"I'm the oldest. You'll get the same privileges when you're my age."

"I doubt it," Martha mumbled.

"You will," Ollie said back.

"All right, girls, that's enough," their mama said. "Martha, you can take the other girls to find that lake once the dishes are washed and the trailer is swept out. Then Gwen can show Ellen how to make those necklaces. Does that sound fair?"

"I don't see how finding one measly lake could make up for . . ."

Reverend Love stepped out of his tent and put an end to Martha's whining. Not by anything he said—they just knew not to squabble in front of their daddy.

A look of relief washed over Susanna's face, and she gave Ollie a gentle push from behind. "Go on, you two," she said. "You've caused enough stirring for one day."

Reverend Love walked over to his wife, pulled her in tightly, and kissed her. Ellen giggled. "We won't be long," he said.

Ollie's mama pushed a shopping list into her daddy's hand. "A few things we can't do without," she said. "Some eggs and maybe one of those cake mixes. Gwen's birthday is almost here. We'd better get the mix while we're near a market."

Reverend Love looked over to Gwen, who was beaming, and winked. "What's your poison?" he asked.

"Chocolate, please," she said.

Gwen always chose chocolate. Ollie's usual choice was carrot with cream cheese frosting. Martha chose pie (which Ollie thought was a complete waste of the birthday dessert privilege). Camille chose their mama's homemade buttermilk cake, and Ellen insisted on cherry chip.

"Chocolate it is!" Reverend Love announced. "And tomorrow," he said, "I'm taking my other girls into town for a soda pop. Ollie will stay home and scrub the breakfast dishes."

Ollie's sisters let out a whoop of joy. Ellen was practically exploding with happiness, and Martha looked something close to pleased. It was true, what Martha said about Ollie getting more privileges than the rest, and Ollie didn't mind doing a few chores to even out the score. If it made living with Martha more bearable, she would willingly wash a cathedral of dishes. Somehow, though, Ollie knew it would never be enough. Martha kept count and always figured the score in Ollie's favor. Poor Martha, thought Ollie, forever counting and never satisfied.

• • •

Ollie was happy to be walking through town at her daddy's side.

"That's the quilting cottage over there. It's run by Mrs. Knuttal." As if her daddy couldn't read the sign. "And the schoolhouse is next on the right. It's a nice town, isn't it?"

"What are you getting at, child?"

"I'm just saying Binder might be a good place to stay for a while. A few extra days, if we have to. That's all."

Her daddy seemed exasperated. "I agreed to give it some thought, Olivene," he said. "I need to talk to the boy first."

"Yes, sir." Ollie decided not to push further.

Moody wasn't on his front porch when they passed by, and no one was at the Koppel place when Ollie and her daddy came up the path. Ollie had warned her daddy—or at least tried to—about what he would see, but nothing could prepare a person for the sight he was to behold at the top of that ridge.

Reverend Love stood on the soft, damp grass at the edge of Jimmy's property and let out a long whistle. It meant, *Wow, look at this mess.* At least, that was Ollie's interpretation.

Ollie walked over to a good-sized woodpile and rolled out two logs. Reverend Love sat down on one and Ollie sat on the other.

"Maybe he's visiting his ma in jail," Ollie said. "Or hunting food for his frogs. He told me he has to catch over six hundred beetles, crickets, and worms every single day—just to keep them fed."

"Maybe," her daddy said.

Ollie was hoping, by the way her daddy set his jaw, that he was working up a plan for helping Jimmy, and since she didn't have a single idea herself, she decided to be quiet and let him think.

"This is a pretty big problem," Reverend Love said.

Ollie watched a tiny brown grasshopper jump across the dirt. "I know it is," she said.

Reverend Love stared out over the field of trash and seemed burdened by what his daughter was asking him to do. "Maybe too big," he said.

"But you're the one always saying there's nothing God can't do."

"It's not God you're asking. It's your mama and me. It's Martha, Gwen, Camille, and Ellen. Helping will come at a price for all of us."

Ollie slid her brown boot through the dust, making a rainbow arc. "So we leave without trying to help him, Daddy? Is that what you're saying?" Her words were soft and low.

Reverend Love thought for a minute and said, "No. I'm just not sure what we can do. Maybe we need to pay a visit to Jimmy's mama."

• • •

Ollie and her daddy headed back down Mason's Holler. A rare breeze danced in the trees and tickled Ollie's neck. She held her daddy's hand and gazed up at the gleaming blue sky.

> "So alone, forlorn and aching,
> Reaching for the reverent light."

Ollie pulled on her daddy's arm and yanked him to a stop. "It's Moody," she said. "The old man I told you about, the one with the satin voice. He must have been inside his house when we passed by before." They were coming back down into the clearing in the Holler.

> "Reach on out, God's love will save you.
> Save your soul, lead you aright."

"That's his song," Ollie said. "Have you ever heard anything so . . ." She couldn't think of how to best describe it. The words were hopeful, but the melody felt like someone was ripping your heart right out of your chest.

"Tender," Reverend Love said.

"Yeah."

"Can't say that I have."

Moody didn't flinch when Ollie and her daddy walked up to his front porch. He was working on carving diamonds into the lid of the same trinket box Ollie had seen before.

"Morning, Ollie," Moody said, not looking up. "This here that preacher daddy you was tellin' me about?"

"Yes, sir," Ollie said. "We missed you at services last night."

"Did you?" Moody carried a lilt in his voice. "I'm sorry to disappoint."

"That's all right. Maybe you'll come tonight."

Moody looked up at the girl and smiled. "You gonna introduce me?"

"Moody, this is my daddy, Reverend Everlasting Love. Daddy, this is Moody. Just Moody."

Reverend Love reached his hand out and said, "Pleasure to meet you, Moody. Do you mind if we sit a spell?"

"No mind," Moody said, scooting over.

"That's beautiful work you have there. Is it maple?" Reverend Love asked.

"Hickory," Moody said. "But you didn't come all the way up here to ask me what kind of wood I whittle."

Reverend Love let out a deep, soft laugh. "No, sir. We didn't. We've come on account of the boy, Jimmy."

"I guessed as much," Moody said.

"Ollie says he's in a real pinch."

"Mmm," Moody said. "Ain't that the truth."

"We'd like to be of some help, if we can." The three sat quiet on Moody's steps, listening to the chickadees twitter and dance in the treetops. Ollie watched Moody's knife twist and turn against the side of his box, allowing thin strips of wood to curl away from the silver blade and float down into a dusty pile at his feet. "Ollie here tells me his mama is in jail," Reverend Love said. "And that Jimmy claims she's an innocent woman."

Moody didn't look up.

"Is it true?" Reverend Love asked.

"Might be," Moody answered.

"What do you think?"

Moody stilled his knife and looked over at Reverend Love. "It didn't have to be her. Lots of folks wanted Henry Koppel dead. Most of Colson County, to tell the truth. That man loved his whiskey bottle and poker cards more than his own kin. He was a mean drunk, too." Moody peered off into the trees and seemed troubled by the thoughts wandering across his mind. "Things he did to that poor woman and her boy . . . it ain't right."

"Do you know how he died?" Ollie broke into the conversation.

"No," Moody said. "Ray Burton, the sheriff's son, found his body in the river. Head bashed in. Now, I did hear Jimmy and his pa hollerin' early that afternoon. Fighting something fierce."

"Do you know what about?" Reverend Love asked.

Moody shrugged. "No, but voices carry over the treetops in this old holler. They was always arguing over something. Nothin' new there."

"Was Henry's body found in this river?" Reverend Love gestured to the creek that ran down the center of the holler and out into a marsh at the bottom.

"That's the one," Moody said. "Though I don't see how Virginia could've done it. Henry Koppel was well over six feet tall and wide as a barn. His wife, Virginia, is a tiny mouse. Timid and weak— sickly, too. That woman can barely lift a cookin' spoon. I don't see how she could have killed Henry and then dragged him all the way to the river." Moody shrugged. "Even so, she confessed and took the punishment."

"But that's not right," Ollie said. "If she didn't do it, why would she confess?"

Moody shook his head. "What's *right* and what *is* don't have nothin' to do with each other. Not a blessed thing."

Reverend Love gave Moody a firm pat on the shoulder. "I appreciate your help."

"No bother," Moody said. "Truth be told, it does me good to think someone might be able to help Jimmy and his mama. They's nice folks. Don't deserve what they've been given. I do what I can to help the boy, but most people in these parts aren't willing to listen to an old man like myself."

Reverend Love stood and reached his hand out to help his daughter up.

"See you tonight?" Ollie asked, full of hope.

Moody shook his head and turned down to his whittling.

"Let's move on," Reverend Love said. "We've taken enough of the gentleman's time."

"But you'd be welcome," Ollie said over her shoulder as her daddy led her down the path to town. "To come, that is."

Moody didn't look up. He was busy whittling and humming another tune—one Ollie hadn't heard yet—and seemed completely lost in his music.

11

Ray Burton sat in a worn-out rocking chair on the porch of his daddy's office. There was a burlap sack filled with sunflower seeds at his side and a pile of chewed, soggy shells around his feet.

"We're here to see Virginia Koppel," Reverend Love said, stepping up onto the porch.

Ray jumped out of the rocker and took a quick leap back against the wall of the building. "Get it away," he said, panicked.

Ollie and her daddy were purely confused.

"Shoo," Ray said, swinging his hands out in wild jets. "Go on, scat."

Ollie turned to notice a mangy cat rubbing its side against the porch rail. It was all bones and fur and she guessed it to be a stray. "This little thing?" she asked.

"Black cat," Ray said, his cheeks flushed with color. "Black as midnight. Black as magic."

Ollie knelt and ran a hand along the cat's back. "He won't harm you none."

Ray wasn't having any of it. He tossed a handful of sunflower seeds, pelting the cat on its head. "Scat!" he said once more, causing it to dart across the road and into a line of leatherleaf bushes.

Ollie had met superstitious people before—they were thick in the South. Still, she couldn't help but feel sorry for that poor cat.

"Can we see Virginia?" Reverend Love asked, bringing the attention back to their reason for being there.

Ray kept his eyes out toward the bush where the cat had fled. "In the basement," he said.

Reverend Love led the way into the sheriff's office and down the narrow staircase to the basement. Two square cells sat side by side, with only slivers of windows along the rear walls—barred, of course. One cell was empty. The other held Virginia Koppel.

"Good morning, Virginia," Ollie's daddy said through the iron bars. "I am Everlasting Love, a preacher from Georgia. My daughter, Ollie here, has become a friend to your boy, Jimmy. I was wondering if I might be able to speak to you."

Virginia Koppel cowered in the corner of her tiny cell. She sat on a pile of matted hay with her legs pulled up to her chest. Moody had been right, she was an itty bit of a woman with frail features and long, stringy hair in the same flat color as the hay around her feet. What Moody hadn't said, however, was anything about her wild, darting eyes and jittery hands, which were rubbed pink and raw from being twisted together.

"Jimmy ain't said nothing about no friend." She was full of suspicion.

Ollie understood Virginia's concern. From what she gathered, no one had shown Virginia even a morsel of kindness, so it was understandable she might not recognize love when it came knocking. "I've only known him a short time, but we've shared a lot," Ollie said. "He's pretty amazing, with all he knows about frogs and—"

"He told you about them frogs?" Virginia asked.

"Sure," Ollie said. "And showed me his ranch."

"That's a lie."

"It is not. He showed me all of it. Rows and rows of those Pure Pak milk cartons, sawed off and made into perfect frog hotels."

Virginia wrapped her arms tight around her knees and tucked her head down like a turtle. "I don't believe it," she said.

"It's the honest-to-goodness truth."

Reverend Love slid on his soothing voice and said, "He's shared other things with Ollie, too. He says you shouldn't be in this cell, Virginia. Jimmy says you're innocent—that you didn't murder your husband. He's asked for our help."

"S'at right?"

"Yes," Ollie said. "Is it true?"

"True?" Virginia laughed. She was a tiny thing, but her laugh was deep and throaty. "What's truth got to do with anything?" She stood up and raised her twiggy arms out to the side. She couldn't have been an inch over five feet tall. "Don't you know who I am? Easy for you to sit out there and talk all high and mighty about what's true and what's not— some traveling preacher bent on fixin' the world. But you can't fix this. As soon as that state prison bus comes, I'll be carted off and my boy will be sent away."

"You didn't answer the question," Reverend Love said with a voice as calm as a summer lake. "Now, Ollie and I tend to believe what Jimmy is saying. We don't see how you could have killed your husband, even if you wanted to."

Virginia was pacing back and forth in her cell, wringing those chapped hands and shaking her head. "No, you're wrong. I done it. Just like they said I did. I killed Henry."

"What do you mean, 'just like they said I did'?"

"Don't go puttin' words in my mouth, preacher man. I said it was me. Wanna know how?"

"Now, Virginia . . ."

"I sneaked up on him while he was sleepin'. I tiptoed real quiet-like up to his bed and raised a skillet over my head." She flung her arms up high. "Then I smacked it down on his skull, mighty as I could. There was blood and brains everywhere." Virginia nodded, satisfied with her performance. "I was alone, too. Just me and Henry."

"Where was Jimmy?" Reverend Love asked.

"Gone somewheres. Huntin' beetles, most likely."

"Uh-huh," Reverend Love said. "And how did a tiny thing like you drag Henry all the way to the river?"

Virginia paused. "Well," she said, "I was angry and full of hatred. Feelin's like that'll give you strength beyond your own."

Reverend Love nodded. "I appreciate your time." He took his daughter by the arm and led her up the stairs.

Reverend Love turned to Ray, who was back in his rocker, still watching the leatherleaf bushes like a hawk. "We thank you," Reverend Love said, tipping his head and starting on down the road.

"That was some confession," Ollie said. "It's no wonder they skipped the trial. I guess Jimmy was wrong."

"No, he was right."

Ollie stopped walking and looked up at her daddy. "But Virginia said she did it. She gave all those awful details."

"Did she once look into our eyes?" Reverend Love asked his daughter.

"No."

"And what was her demeanor?"

"She was uneasy. You're right, she didn't do it after all!"

"Someone killed Henry Koppel, but it was not her."

"So we'll stay?"

"We'll stay."

"For as long as it takes?"

"I can't promise that," Reverend Love said. "One day, one step at a time. That'll have to be enough."

And for Ollie, it was.

12

Jimmy was standing in a field of green and purple kudzu, petting a sheep. Ollie saw him as they came down the road from the sheriff's office.

"There he is, Daddy."

Reverend Love stepped over the three-rail fence and walked out toward the boy. Ollie had to run to keep up with his long legs.

"Ollie," Jimmy said with a short nod when they came to him.

"Hi, Jimmy. We missed you at services last night."

"I was busy feeding my frogs," Jimmy said.

Ollie smiled at the thought of Jimmy's frog ranch. "This here is my daddy, the good Reverend Everlasting Love. He's gonna help us find a way to free your mama."

"You told him?"

"I had to. That's what daddies are for." The

moment the words jumped off her tongue, she was sorry.

Reverend Love reached down and playfully tugged on a lamb's ear. "This your flock, son?"

"No."

"Mind if we sit a spell? My old legs could use a rest."

Jimmy shrugged.

"My wife grew up with a few sheep on her land," Reverend Love said as he pulled one of the lambs over and ran his hand through the wool. "I guess she went from living with one kind of shepherd to another."

"Yes, sir," Jimmy said.

Reverend Love looked up at the boy. "Are you going to stand over me this whole time?"

Jimmy sat down.

"There are several hundred breeds of sheep. Did you know that?"

"No, sir."

"It'd take your whole life to learn them all." Reverend Love ran a finger along a kudzu vine that roped and twisted across the ground. He gazed out over the field and then turned to Jimmy. "'Bout the same with folks, I'd say. We may seem different on the outside, but we're really not. We're all looking for that flock to welcome us home."

"I'm not sure what you're getting at," Jimmy said.

"I'm saying that you and I are more alike than you realize. We all breathe the same air, feel the same sun, and sleep under the same moon. We laugh and cry and bleed. It only makes sense we would both want the same thing for your mama. That we would both understand the truth."

Jimmy hesitated.

Ollie could see his heart struggle with his desire for help and his fear of the unknown. "We visited your mama," she said. "We came from the jail just now."

"What'd she tell you?"

"That she killed your daddy. Likely the same story she told Sheriff Burton, but we don't believe her, Jimmy. We know it's not true."

Jimmy looked long and hard at both Ollie and her daddy. "Do you think anything can be done?" he asked.

"Well, we can start by learning what you know," Reverend Love said. "You need to tell me everything, son. What happened on the day your daddy died?"

Jimmy dipped his head down. "I don't know, exactly. I wasn't there."

"Where were you?"

"My daddy and I got into an argument, so I left

to clear my head. When I came home, Mama was sittin' in her rocker with a wet cloth on her head. Blood was spillin' out from a gash above her eye, trickling down her arm." Jimmy's face was dark with the memory of that day. "We didn't know he was dead until the sheriff told us. We figured he'd run off drinkin' again."

"Was your daddy the one who hurt your mama?" Reverend Love asked.

"Yeah," Jimmy said. His voice turned sharp and angry. "Like always."

Ollie reached out for Jimmy's hand. He pulled it away.

"But I know what she's sayin' is a lie 'cuz there wasn't no blood in their bed. No blood on the pillow, or the blankets. No blood on the floor where she would have had to drag him out. How could she lift him anyway?"

"The sheriff didn't notice that?" Ollie asked.

"As if he even looked. He came and told us they found my daddy's body down by the river and that they were gonna take one of us to jail. That's when Mama confessed."

"Who do you think could have killed him?" Reverend Love asked.

Jimmy scoffed. "You got a phone book? That'd

be your list of suspects. My daddy was the worst kind. He traveled to the different towns along the highway. He owed money, and had girlfriends . . ." His voice trailed off.

"All right, that's a start. Maybe you could write up a list of folks your daddy knew, gambling buddies and such, and bring it to me tonight. Could you do that?"

Jimmy kept looking down to the ground. "I don't know any names."

"Not a single one?"

"No, sir."

"Son, are you trying to tell me you can't think of one name?"

Jimmy pressed his lips into a tight line. "No," he said.

• • •

The bell that hung above the door to Carter's Fresh rang when Ollie and her daddy entered. Esther Carter stood by the cash register, counting out piles of pennies.

"Help ya?" she asked.

Reverend Love waved the list his wife gave him in the air. "Picking up a few things."

Any other shopkeeper would have gone back to counting pennies and allowed the customers to do their shopping, but not Mrs. Carter. Her fingers kept moving through the lines of coins, but her eyes stayed glued on Ollie and the reverend.

"You don't believe him, right?" Ollie whispered to her daddy.

Reverend Love looked up to the front of the store, where Mrs. Carter was straining her ears, and gave his daughter a warning look.

"But you don't, do you?" Ollie mouthed.

Reverend Love shook his head at his daughter. "There's no-thing like fresh eggs," he said, taking a carton and putting it in the handbasket he picked up at the front of the store.

Ollie noticed how he said "no-thing" and took it as her answer. She thought it funny, so added, "Cake mix, too. No-thing like delicious chocolate cake."

They went on like that—likely annoying the cotton drawers off Mrs. Carter—as they added items to the basket.

"No-thing like cooking oil," Ollie said.

"No-thing like a dusting of sugar to make the cake pretty," her daddy replied.

When they took their provisions up to the checkout, Mrs. Carter waved a tobacco-stained finger at them and said, "I'll give you this warning. Folks 'round here don't take kindly to strangers with too many questions."

"Speak plainly," Reverend Love said.

"Virginia Koppel deserves to be in that jail. Them's no-good thievin' folks who never caused nothin' but trouble 'round here."

Reverend Love rubbed his chin. "I'd agree that description might fit Henry Koppel, at least what I've learned of him. But I'd hardly say it fits Virginia or the boy."

"They's one 'n' the same. A Koppel's a Koppel. The Bible itself says the apple don't fall far from the tree."

"Well, there *is* fruit mentioned in scripture," Reverend Love said, "but I'm afraid you are remembering it incorrectly."

Esther Carter handed the reverend his change. "My point's the same. You'd be wise to leave well enough alone when it comes to that matter."

Ollie couldn't hold her tongue. "But Sheriff Burton never did an investigation. How could Virginia have clubbed her husband's brains out while he was sleeping if there wasn't even any blood in the bed?"

Reverend Love steadied his daughter with a gentle touch to her arm. "I believe we're finished here."

"Don't need no investigatin'," Mrs. Carter called out as the two left the store. "A confession is a confession."

13

Reverend Love took his daughter by Jeb Marshall's house on their way back to the preaching field. It was their third day in Binder and the original agreement would have the Love family pulling out at sunrise the following day.

Mr. Marshall kept behind his screen door, making it a challenge to see his face. "Reverend," he said in greeting. "I appreciate you coming with my portion from last night."

Ollie's daddy reached into his pocket and pulled out a small fold of bills. He peeled one off and held it up. Jeb Marshall reached a hand out, grabbed the money, and let the screen door fall shut.

So much for Southern hospitality.

"I was hoping to talk to you about staying on a few more days," Reverend Love said.

"Is this regarding the Koppel boy?" Mr. Marshall asked.

"And his mother, yes," Reverend Love said.

Mr. Marshall shifted behind the gray screen. "I think it's time for your family to be moving on."

"I don't understand the problem," Reverend Love said.

"Your daughter there has caused quite a stir, going up Mason's Holler and asking questions about that boy and his mama. My wife and I don't need trouble with our neighbors."

"No harm in a few questions," Reverend Love said.

"You've made your point and I've made mine."

"Is there any room for discussion?"

"My mind is set. I'm willing to honor my original agreement, but you need to be off my land at daybreak."

Mr. Marshall's shadow turned and faded back into his living room. Esther Carter's words jumped into Ollie's head. *Jeb Marshall ain't never done nothing without earning a profit in the matter.* She tugged on her daddy's shirtsleeve and whispered, "Offer him more money."

Her daddy gave her a questioning look, but Ollie nodded and mouthed, "More money."

"Might I offer you a bigger cut?" Reverend Love called out.

Mr. Marshall's face appeared behind the screen again. "Keep talkin'," he said.

"What will it take?" Ollie jumped in. She knew she was out of line, but was feeling desperate. She didn't care if they made another penny in Binder. She wanted more time to sort things out with Jimmy and his mama.

"Eighty percent," Mr. Marshall said. "For eighty percent, you can stay as long as you want."

• • •

Reverend Love walked his daughter back over to the camp area, where her mama and sisters were waiting. Ollie knew her daddy would explain everything to her sisters—in time—but she also knew he'd start with his wife. He led Susanna into their tent for a private discussion.

"Wanna see my dandelion necklace?" Ellen asked, her face bright with hope. "Gwen taught me today, like she promised."

"Sure," Ollie said.

Ellen reached into her pinafore pocket and pulled out a wadded-up ball of stems and broken flowers.

"Oh, Ellen," Ollie said, full of compassion, "you can't keep it in there, it'll get all crumbled."

Ellen's bottom lip pushed out and started trembling. Tears rimmed her soft hazel eyes. "I didn't know," she said in a shaky whisper. "No one told me."

Martha and Camille were pulling dresses from a white wicker basket and pinning them on the wash line. "For heaven's sake, Ellen," Martha scolded. "You're nearly six years old. We shouldn't have to tell you *everything.*"

"It's okay, Ellen," Ollie soothed her baby sister as she darted an angry look at Martha. "Why don't you go ask Gwen to help you make another one, and this time we'll hang it from the nail on the tent post so it stays safe."

"Gwen's reading her Bible," Ellen whimpered. "She's busy."

"Then I'll help you." Ollie took Ellen's hand and walked out to the patch of dandelions that was nestled between long stalks of rye grass in the middle of the field. "Now that you know how to make the necklaces," Ollie said, "it'll go real fast and you can make as many as you want, whenever you want."

Ellen smiled at the prospect.

The two girls sat across from each other and farmed yellow blossoms out of the ground. Ollie hummed "When the Saints Go Marching In," and Ellen poked her pink tongue out of the corner of her mouth in concentration as she made her new necklace.

It was hot, that went without saying. Rivers of sweat trickled down Ollie's neck and tickled the back of her ears. She sat up and twisted her long hair into a knot. "You know something, Ellen," she began. "People all over the world can walk into their kitchens and pull ready-made ice from their freezers."

"Oh," Ellen said. "I'd like that."

"Whenever they get a hankering for something cold, there it is, ready for the taking."

"I'd fill a bathtub with ice if I had my own freezer," Ellen said.

"Not me," Ollie said. "It'd melt all at once and be wasted. You know what I'd do?"

"What?" Ellen was enchanted. She leaned forward and rested her chin on the soft palm of her hand, looking dreamily up toward her big sister.

"I'd take one piece at a time and slowly run it all over my forehead, down past my ear, then across the back of my neck—"

"And that hot, sticky place behind your knees!"

"And I'd drink iced lemonade all the livelong day," Ollie added.

"Would you invite me over and share your iced lemonade?"

"You bet," Ollie said. "That's the power of electricity."

Ellen gave a satisfied smile. "The power of electricity. That sounds real nice."

"It's better than nice, Ellen. It's a *modern convenience.*"

"Oooh," Ellen crooned. Then she tilted her head in question. "But what about the preaching, Ollie? You'd keep to the road, right?"

Ollie pressed her lips together and fiddled with the blossoms in her lap.

"Ollie?" Ellen asked again.

"The preaching road isn't so great when you're thirteen," Ollie said. "You don't understand that now, because you're five."

"Five is a lot."

"I know. Still, it's different for me."

"But we're a family," Ellen said, her voice a little timid.

"Yes, Ellen. We're a family." Ollie didn't want to worry her baby sister, not that there was any point to their conversation anyway. A preaching family is what they were.

Reverend Love's whistle cut through the stagnant afternoon heat.

"We'd better get back," Ollie said, leading her sister over to the preaching canopy, where her daddy gathered the family. Reverend Love sat on a chair. Camille, Gwen, and Martha sat with their legs crossed by his feet, and their mama stood behind him, with her hands placed on his shoulders.

"Girls," Reverend Love began in his preaching voice. "We've a purpose in this town. I do believe God Himself has led us here. He needs us, and there are some other souls who need us, too."

"Do they need us to preach the word, Daddy?" Gwen asked, ready to rise to the occasion.

"Not exactly, though there's always opportunity for that." Reverend Love went on to tell his girls what his oldest daughter, and now his wife, knew—about how Jimmy's mama was an innocent woman and how she didn't have a single soul to stand up for her. He told them about his visit to the Koppel place (although Ollie noted he didn't elaborate on the extent of the mess found there) and how Moody told him no one in Binder would help a Koppel, innocent or not. "Ollie has convinced me there is a need to stay here a while longer. Truth is not being honored. If we don't help this poor woman and her child, who will?" Reverend Love asked his family. "You know we've always kept to ourselves when it came to the politics of towns and families. We preach our message, try to give a measure of joy, and then move on. But this is different. Can you see that, girls?"

Ellen was nodding so hard her head nearly bobbled off her neck and rolled across the field.

Gwen looked pensive and deeply concerned for the welfare of both Jimmy and his mama. "Should we offer them a hot meal?" she asked.

"Good thinking," Reverend Love said. "I'm sure your mama is already making plans along those lines." Then he slapped his hands on his thighs and said, "Let's get things rolling for services."

"Do you think anyone will come?" Martha asked.

Trouble lined the preacher's brow. "I hope so," he said.

"Hope," Camille chimed in. "To desire with one's heart."

"That's right," Reverend Love said, pulling Camille into his side. "Hope has to do with the heart."

• • •

Only a handful of people made their way out to the field that evening. One was Mrs. Mahoney, who brought a pocketful of peppermints and new riddles to share with the Love girls. The others included a husband and wife who happened to be passing through Binder on their way to Little Rock for a seed-corn convention, Paul Monson of Monson's Insurance, and some friends Ellen had made. The last to come was Jimmy.

"Glad you made it," Ollie said when Jimmy sat down next to her on Nana Shirlene's patchwork quilt. He hadn't done much to clean up for the occasion. Combing his hair appeared to be the extent of it.

Reverend Love began the service. Ollie thought it awkward singing and preaching to a few lonely souls sitting under a canopy in the middle of a vast and open field, but her daddy acted like it was the most normal thing in the world. Susanna sat down next to Jimmy, patting his knee and smiling her smile and echoing every single one of his amens. Ollie was certain there wasn't a person alive who could make a soul feel more welcome than her mama could.

And Jimmy did feel welcome. He sang the songs and raised a worshipping hand. He bowed his head and called amen. It was a beautiful sight to see the joy coming from somewhere deep inside of him. The joy that comes when you finally let go of the worry and settle down into the comfort of friends.

When it was over, the offering basket held a paltry two dollars and seventy-three cents, two eighteen of which would go to Jeb Marshall.

"You come early for supper tomorrow, you hear?" Susanna said to Jimmy as he was getting ready to leave.

"I wouldn't miss it."

Ollie walked Jimmy out to the edge of the field. Night was coming on, and she only had a few minutes to talk before her mama would call her back.

"Thanks again for coming," she said.

Jimmy looked over to the camp where the Love family was gathered around the wash bucket. "You're so lucky," he said. "To have such a family."

How could Ollie tell Jimmy it wasn't so great? That she hated living on the road, even if it was with good people? "Nothing's perfect," she decided to say.

Jimmy kept his gaze on the camp. "Seems pretty close to me," he said.

"Jimmy," Ollie began, "how come you won't write that list of suspects for my daddy?"

"I told you. I don't know any names."

"I don't believe you. My daddy doesn't believe you either."

Jimmy looked far off across the field. "I can't give you no list."

"Why not?"

"Can't, that's all. You gotta accept that."

Jimmy turned and walked off across the field. Ollie rubbed her tired face and took a long, deep breath before going back to her family.

• • •

"Everything all right?" Ollie's mama asked when she got back.

"Fine," Ollie said.

The air seemed heavy and thick as they finished cleaning up the field and getting ready for bed. "The right choice isn't always the easy choice," Reverend Love said to no one and everyone at the same time.

Ollie gave her daddy a knowing smile.

"Tell me, Martha," Reverend Love continued in his effort to ease the tension, "did you find that lake today?"

Martha looked over to Ollie. "Sure did," she said. "It was a grand one, too."

"Was not," Ellen said from under her mama's braiding hands. "It wasn't nothin' but no mud puddle."

"They call it Pollywog Pond," Gwen offered, "but we didn't see no pollywogs."

"*Any* pollywogs," Susanna Love said, not slowing her hands from twisting.

"Nope, but we did see lots of pond scum," Gwen said.

"And rocks," Ellen added.

"And that black, stinky mud."

"All right," Martha said. "You've made your point. It's July, for heaven's sake! I bet it's grand in the spring, just like it shows in my map book."

"I bet it is," Ollie said with pure intentions.

"Oh shut up," Martha said.

"Martha!" Susanna Love gasped.

"I'm sorry, Mama, but Ollie acts like she's so high and mighty when she's only eleven months older than me. Not even a full year! How come she gets a special date to go into town with Daddy? How come you're inviting her friend for dinner? How come she gets to determine where we stay and for how long? It's not right."

Everyone stood silent. Even Susanna's hands stilled at the very end of Ellen's braid.

"Well," Reverend Love said, holding his voice low and steady, "I suppose, as the head of this family, I get to choose what's right and what's not. I don't recall promising to keep things perfectly even or perfectly fair among you girls, but I do believe that, in the end, you all get your share of good things." Then he looked right at Martha. "Do you not?"

"Yes, sir," Martha said.

"Because I seem to remember promising to take you for a soda pop tomorrow. And I also recall lingering at the Mississippi River two whole hours so a certain someone could find the right kind of rocks to mark off in her travel journal."

"Yes, sir."

"Shall I continue?"

"No, sir."

"Then I'll say good night."

Susanna worked quick braids through the rest of her girls' hair. When her mama was finished, Ollie followed her sisters into the trailer, where they turned down the lantern, slid into their blankets, and fell asleep without a word.

14

Not long after Ollie fell asleep, she awoke to the sharp crack of wood breaking and two thumping feet running away. She sat up in her bed and leaned over to look out the window. A sunny glow was lighting the day outside, but Ollie knew it was no-where near morning. She stood up to get a closer look and saw flames crackling and flickering against the glass.

"Fire," she gasped. She tried to suck in a breath to scream, but couldn't get her lungs to work. They had gone tight within her chest and wouldn't let any air in. Ollie began slapping her sisters' blankets. "Fire," she said in a hoarse whisper. "Get up, fire!"

"Hey," Martha moaned. "I'm sleeping."

Camille appeared at Ollie's side. "Fire!" she screamed. "Manifestation of light, flame, and heat! Passion!"

"Yes," Ollie said, pushing her sister toward the door. "Light and heat. Out! Everyone out!"

That's when the world broke loose. Ellen caught a glimpse of the flames licking the window and started screaming like holy murder. The trailer door flew open and Reverend Love jumped in, scooping all five girls into his two arms and pulling them outside into the field of rye grass, which was building into blazes. The family pushed through the stifling black smoke that was rolling up in pillars to the sky.

Flames skipped all around them in a wicked dance. The heat and pressure of the fire pushed against Ollie's skin, making it feel tight and sunburned. She lifted her hand to her braid, holding it tightly and praying it wouldn't catch a spark and go up in flames like the whole world around her.

"My Baby Doll Sue," Ellen began bellowing into the night. "She's in the trailer! She'll burn up, I know it!" She wriggled out of her daddy's grip and darted back toward the fire to save her doll. Susanna ran after Ellen, lifted her up in her arms, and whispered soothing words into her ear.

"Baby Doll Sue," Ellen was wailing like all getout. "My Baby Doll Sue."

Once they were a safe distance out into the field, where the air was fresh and cool, Reverend Love began counting heads. "Ollie, Martha, Camille . . . Ellen. Where's Gwen?"

Panic flashed across Susanna Love's face as she slid Ellen off her lap and stood up, peering back into the night. Blistering flames were consuming the parents' tent and moving underneath the travel trailer. "Gwen!" she hollered. "Oh Sweet Lord, Gwen!"

Ellen's sobs immediately turned from "Baby Doll Sue" to "Gwen."

"I'm going back in," Reverend Love said.

"Oh, Everlasting!" Susanna cried.

"She's over here," Martha called from farther into the field.

Everyone hurried over to where Martha was standing. Gwen was kneeling down in the tall grass, eyes shut tight, mumbling a fervent prayer. Reverend Love dropped to his knees. Susanna and Ollie followed. They all said their own words—crying out their own hearts' desires. Ollie began praying for Jimmy and Virginia Koppel, and she could overhear her mama right next to her saying a prayer of thanks for all her girls being safe. Reverend Love was praying for peace and long-suffering, but Gwen was praying for something different. Gwen was praying for rain. Ollie thought that was the best idea for a prayer yet, so she joined Gwen in the plea for a summer storm. Soon the whole Love family was on bended knee, begging heaven for raindrops.

And they came. First it was just a few. Ellen felt one strike the top of her head and jumped up, singing, "Rain, rain, rain."

Ollie turned her face up to the heavens as two fat drops splatted across her left cheek. "She's right," Ollie said. "It is raining."

Within minutes, scattered drops turned into hundreds, and hundreds turned into thousands. Hot summer rain sheeted out of the night sky in torrents, drenching the family as they laughed and sang and embraced each other out in the field of God's simplicity.

15

Morning was a soggy mess. The fire took Reverend and Susanna Love's sleeping tent, along with the laundry line full of clothes and two wooden stools. By the grace of God, their travel trailer and preaching canopy had been spared.

The family sorted through the remains, separating what was completely ruined from what might be redeemable. The parents' sleeping bags and cots were a lost cause, but a few of Susanna Love's dresses could likely be washed and mended.

Ollie caught a glimpse of her daddy out of the corner of her eye and watched as he walked over to what was left of his nightstand. He kneeled down on the blackened earth and ran his fingers through a heap of ashes and charred leather scraps. Everyone fell silent as they realized he was touching the remains of what was once his granddaddy's Bible. The one that had been passed down from generation to generation. The one his own daddy handed him right before he let out his last breath and died.

Ollie lived thirteen years without seeing her daddy cry, but she saw it happen that morning. He lifted the remains of the old book in his great hands, dropped his head, and sobbed.

"Here, Daddy," Gwen said at his side, voice wavering. "You can take my Bible. I know it's not the same on the outside, but the words are all there. The lessons are the same. Really, Daddy," she said. "It's yours now."

Reverend Love didn't look up. Gwen dipped her sweet face down and turned back toward the trailer.

Ollie went to her daddy. She knelt next to him and gently lifted the burned Bible scraps from his hands. The leather was blistered and crumbled when she touched it. "Oh, Daddy," she said. "I'm so sorry." She wanted to say more. She ached to tell him they were making the right decision staying in Binder and that it would all work out, but she couldn't bring herself to do it. That Bible meant everything to her daddy.

Every single thing.

Reverend Love gave a nod and stood up.

Susanna wrapped her arms around her husband's

waist and snuggled into his chest. He looked out across the camp once more and said, "I'm going to see the sheriff."

Susanna picked up the pieces of their family Bible, wrapped them in a scrap of dress fabric, and set the bundle tenderly on the charred aluminum folding table.

Reverend Love headed into town.

Ellen was clueless and happy. Her Baby Doll Sue had survived the fire without harm inside their trailer. The doll was tucked tightly into a blanket sling that was tied around her shoulders. Ellen was singing,

"Mama's little baby loves short'nin', short'nin'
Mama's little baby loves short'nin' bread."

She kept singing those two lines over and over and over until Martha told her to hush.

The night rain had passed, and a shimmering silver-blue sky stretched out tight and wide over Ollie's head. She looked up at that gorgeous sky and marveled at how fresh and innocent it seemed—how oblivious it was to the terrible night they had endured.

Ollie looked to Gwen, who was sitting on the trailer step, head hung low. She walked over to her sister. "He wasn't trying to ignore you," she said.

Gwen looked up, her dark lashes heavy with tears. "Yes he was," she said. "He didn't even see me."

"You know that's not true. Daddy loves you, Gwen."

"Maybe." She lifted her hem to her eyes and blotted the tears. "But he would have listened to me if I were a boy."

"You don't know that."

"Don't I? If I were a boy, my words would be more important. He'd let me shadow him—teach me the trade. He'd see me, Ollie. At the heart."

"I see you, Gwen."

Gwen pointed to where their mama stood. "Don't worry about me," she said in classic Gwen form.

Ollie reached down and gave her sister a hug. "Why don't you talk to him?" she whispered in her ear.

Gwen lifted a single shoulder and forced a smile. "Go to Mama while I help Martha sort the clothes."

Ollie walked over to the fire pit and lifted a half-burned dress out of her mama's hands. "Let me do this for you. Why don't you sit a spell while I get some water boiling for a cup of tea."

Susanna moved without expression over to a stump that was propped by the fire circle and sat down next to Camille. Ollie placed their blue and white speckled kettle on the grate that crossed the campfire. She put a chamomile tea bag from the tin canister into a mug.

"It's a miracle, don't you think?" Ollie said in an effort to focus on the good and remind her mama to do the same. "The rain? Who knew Gwen could call down a storm?" Her voice was high and chatty, even though she was trying to sound calm. "It's a true miracle."

Susanna stared off across the long field.

"And an old pup tent is easy to replace," Ollie continued. "Much easier than the trailer would be—or the big preaching canopy. I bet that would cost a pretty penny to replace. How much was that canopy anyway?"

"Why don't you shut up, Ollie," Martha said as she tromped by with a load of dress scraps draped across her arm. "No one is talking to you."

"You are," Ollie said.

Martha kept walking.

Ollie turned back to her mama, fully expecting Martha to be chastised, but it wasn't going to happen. Mama didn't even hear her girls squabbling. Camille sat at her side, arms wrapped around her waist, and snuggled into her shoulder. She wasn't offering any definitions for loss or sorrow or grief.

Ellen tugged on Ollie's dress from behind. "I ain't mad at you, Ollie," she said. "And Baby Doll Sue ain't mad either."

"Thanks, Ellen," Ollie said. She bent over and gave Ellen a kiss on the cheek. Then Ellen lifted up her baby doll for a kiss, too. Ollie obliged and said, "You see the miracle, don't you, Baby Doll Sue?"

Ellen held the baby doll to her ear and answered, "She said yes."

Ollie pulled the kettle from the fire and poured some tea. She gently wrapped her mama's hands around the warm mug. "Here you go," she said.

Ollie's mama held the mug, but didn't move it to her lips. Ollie stood over her for a moment and let out a ragged breath, turning back to the mess of black ashes that was once her parents' tent. They'd need to be raked into a pile and buried or carted off.

"Mrs. Mahoney's here!" Ellen shouted, running out to meet her.

Mrs. Mahoney came into camp and sat down next to Camille and Susanna. "I saw your daddy in town and he told me what happened." Her words were delicate and flowing. "Everything's going to be all right." She patted Susanna on the knee. Susanna took quick hold of Mrs. Mahoney's hand and held on tight. Like their entire world depended on the woman's promise.

"It could have been worse," Ollie said, bringing

up the positive again. "Trailer's fine. And us, too. That's most important."

"Course it is, dear," Mrs. Mahoney said, keeping tight hold of Susanna's hand.

"Daddy'll sort it all out with the sheriff."

"Doesn't matter," Mrs. Mahoney said. "What's done is done."

Ollie was surprised to see her daddy lumbering across the field and glanced over at her mama, who perked up and managed a small smile. "He's back so soon," Ollie said.

Ellen and Camille ran across the scalded patches of grass to meet their daddy, but Ollie, Martha, and Gwen held back. It was as if they were suddenly too old to skitter out in the field with the other children—as if they had grown up overnight.

With girls hanging from his arms and legs, Reverend Love walked back into camp. He playfully plucked Ellen off his leg and threw her at least five feet into the air. She giggled with delight when he caught her and plunked her back down at his feet. "Me next, me next," Camille shouted. Ollie was happy to see her sisters' mood change so quickly. Maybe that gave hope for them all. She smiled and thought how most other daddies couldn't toss their five- and eight-year-old girls up into the sky, but Reverend Love wasn't like most other daddies. He was strong and let his two youngest have their fill of being tossed.

• • •

Reverend Love explained that Sheriff Burton didn't give a rat's tail about their camp being burned to the ground. He said the sheriff accused the family of being careless with their lanterns and denied anyone in Binder had been out to the field. He even said the family was lucky none of Mr. Marshall's property was permanently damaged and that, if it had been, there would be charges. Ollie knew her daddy was pretty upset when he used the phrase *rat's tail*. It wasn't like him to speak that way.

"Maybe we should go," Susanna said. "Maybe this isn't a safe place for our family to be." Her voice was shaking.

Ollie glanced at her mama's troubled face and then over to her daddy. She understood her mama's concern, but couldn't imagine walking away from Jimmy now. The twist of her daddy's eyebrows let her know he was thinking the same. "But what about the boy, Susanna? We can't leave him."

"We'll take him with us. Let's go—get away from this place."

"We'd be taking him away from everything he knows, from his own ma." Reverend Love took his wife's hand in his. "It doesn't seem right." He looked into her eyes and brushed his thumb across her soft cheek. Then he turned to his girls. "Besides," he said, "I'm not afraid. Who's afraid?"

"Not me," Ollie said, resolved.

"Not me," Ellen chimed in, and then she began chirping, "Not me, not me, not me."

"Gwen? Martha? Camille?" Reverend Love asked. "Are you girls afraid?"

Gwen smiled at her daddy and said, "No. I'm not afraid."

Ollie marveled at how readily Gwen set aside her feelings to help another.

"Afraid," Camille said. "Filled with fear." She mulled over the words, twisting her lips into a knot. "Nope. I guess not. Not filled, anyway." That made even her mama smile.

"Martha?" Reverend Love asked.

"I'd just as soon move on. If we head northwest, I could mark off the Ozarks in my map book."

Reverend Love lowered his voice the tiniest bit. "The question was if you were afraid to stay."

"No," Martha said, not hiding her disappointment. "I'm not."

Reverend Love turned victoriously toward his wife. "See? No worries."

"I don't know," Susanna said.

"Susanna has a point," Mrs. Mahoney said. She was giving tender pats to Camille's hand. "Your sweet family can't stay in this field. I doubt old Jeb would agree, even if you wanted to. Why don't you all move into my home for the rest of your stay?"

"It's a mighty kind offer, but we wouldn't want to bring any trouble your way," Reverend Love said.

"I've been living in this town since before it was on a map. Heavens, I used to tend Tommy Burton's mama back when she was an itty-bitty thing in pigtails. Bring your family into my home, Reverend Love. There will not be any trouble."

Ellen threw her arms around Mrs. Mahoney's legs, nearly toppling the old woman.

"Thank you. Your offer is more than kind," Reverend Love said. Then he turned to Ollie. "Why don't you take your mama into town today? I think it's time she met Virginia firsthand. It might help her understand why we need to stay."

"Yes, sir," Ollie said.

Reverend Love turned to his other girls. "Let's clean up this mess and get packing."

16

Susanna insisted on taking a bundle of biscuits to Virginia. They always kept their leftovers in the trailer, so the biscuits had been spared from the fire. As they walked into town, Ollie realized how beautiful that spot of Arkansas was. Wildflowers and sweet grasses dressed the breeze with their tender scents. Perfect squares of farmland marked out the earth like God's own crossword puzzle. For once, the sun was being nice and tucked itself behind a cotton cloud, which cooled things a bit. Ollie slipped her hand into her mama's and gave a gentle squeeze. Susanna looked at her oldest daughter with a hesitant smile.

"You'll see," Ollie said. "And then you'll know."

When they passed through Binder, folks came out onto their porches. Esther Carter stood in front of her market, arms folded smugly across her chest.

Ollie cut her eyes to the woman and gave the very best scowl she could manage.

Joseph Carter came across the road, blocking their path. Susanna stepped around the boy, smiling her easy smile and dipping her chin as she strolled past him. "Afternoon," she said, sweet as she could. If something was bothering her, he would never know it.

Was it you in the field last night? Ollie wondered, glaring at the boy as she led her mama farther down the street.

Ray Burton was sitting on the steps of his daddy's office. *Maybe it was you?* Ollie wondered as she came closer to him. *Were those the boots I heard running away from the fire?*

"Help ya?" Ray asked.

"We're here to see Virginia Koppel," Ollie said.

"S'at right?" Ray popped a handful of sunflower seeds into his mouth, chewed them around, and spit the broken shells out onto the ground. A chunk of black, slimy shell landed on Ollie's shoe. She shook it off.

"You can't stop us. We have a right," Ollie said.

"Who's stoppin' you?"

Ollie looked to her mama and then stepped around Ray and into the sheriff's office. No one was at the desk, which was a thing she was grateful for, so she showed her mama down the stairwell that led to the jail cells.

Virginia Koppel was sitting on her pile of filthy matted hay in the corner of her cell. She looked just as tired and frightened as Ollie remembered.

"Hello, Mrs. Koppel," Ollie said when they came into the room. "This here's my mama, Susanna Love."

Ollie could see her mama was moved by the tiny woman. "I brought you some buttermilk biscuits," Susanna said. "They're yesterday's batch. Our morning didn't lend itself to baking, I'm sorry to say."

Virginia Koppel stood up and snatched the biscuits quick as a wink. "Much 'bliged," she said as she sat on the ground and wolfed down the biscuits in three bites.

"Do they feed you much in here?" Susanna asked, taking in the sight around her. The cell was dank and dreary, with a bitter-sharp stench that lingered in the air, and Ollie fought a powerful urge to pinch her nose shut. She noticed a waste bucket in the corner and thought it was likely the source of the foul smell. She couldn't imagine Sheriff Burton being in a hurry to clean it out.

Virginia licked her pointer finger and dabbed every crumb of biscuit up off her skirt. "Some," she said. "Mostly leavings."

"Trash?" Ollie asked. Her mama shot her a look. "Sorry," she said.

"No mind," Virginia said. "I know what it is. Truth be told, it ain't all bad. Cucumber peelin's can be sweet, and the boy brings a fresh chicken leg on occasion—if his pa ain't spyin'."

"Ray does that?" Ollie asked.

"He's got compassion, that one," Virginia said. "Christian character, as you folks call it."

Susanna sat down on the wooden bench on the free side of the cell. "We've come to help," she said, and Ollie knew it was true.

"Can't help me none," Virginia said. "'Cept maybe you bring me some more of dem biscuits— if'n you get leftovers."

"All right," Susanna said, "I'll keep that in mind. Now, I wonder if you might tell me who killed your husband." She said it as calm and sweet as if she was asking where Mrs. Koppel bought butter or if she liked to pepper her cornbread.

Ollie fully expected Virginia to recount the same confession she shared before, but Virginia sat quiet. She rocked herself back and forth and twisted her chapped hands around each other.

"We've already spoken to your boy in great detail," Susanna said. "He's told us everything."

"Everything?" Virginia asked.

"Yes. It's a good boy you raised in Jimmy. You should be proud of him."

Virginia gave a single nod, opened her mouth, closed it, and then opened it once again. "Pert' near everyone wanted Henry dead."

"Then you don't know who killed him?" Susanna asked.

Virginia was silent for another long moment. "When I come to, Henry was gone. Later they found his body in the river. Head bloodied."

"I see," Ollie's mama said. "Jimmy told us Henry hurt you that day, but I need to hear it from your own mouth, Virginia."

"He knocked me out cold."

If Susanna was shocked, she didn't show it. Ollie kept darting her eyes from her mama to Mrs. Koppel and back again, like she was watching a game of Ping-Pong. What changed Virginia's mind about telling her story? This hardly seemed to be the same woman Ollie and her daddy visited the day before. Ollie was baffled by these two women sitting across from each other chatting about wife-beating and bloodied heads like they were exchanging pie-crust recipes.

Virginia shook her head sharply, trying to pry

free the memory of that day. "On account of the boy," she said.

"The fight," Ollie said, remembering what Moody had told them. "Jimmy and his daddy had an argument."

"That's right," Virginia went on. "The boy was powerfully upset. His pa played a mean trick of boilin' up some frogs for lunch and then offerin' the soup to him. Didn't tell him what he was eatin' 'til it was gone—lied and said it was possum stew. Jimmy et up five of his favorites, even the one with the yellow and green eyes. Those are his pets, like babes to him. His pa laughed and laughed. It wasn't nice what he done. After Jimmy run off, I spoke against Henry and he came at me." Her gaze fell on her hands, twisting and squirming in her lap. "I shouldn't have spoken out," she said in a whisper. "I might have known what would come of it."

"Thank you for telling me this." Susanna stood and reached a hand through the bars.

"I don't want no trouble for Jimmy," his ma pleaded, taking Susanna's hand. "Best you drop it."

It wasn't until Virginia said those words that Ollie knew why the woman signed that confession. She didn't kill her husband, but she knew who did. It was the only person this side of heaven she'd go to jail for. It was Jimmy.

• • •

Ollie's mouth was dry as chalk as they made their way back to the field. On one hand, she was mad at Jimmy for killing his daddy and then allowing his mama to rot in jail for the crime. On the other hand, she understood why he did it. If Virginia jumped in and confessed to the crime, Sheriff Burton likely wasn't asking too many questions.

Lord, that boy was in a terrible predicament.

"She only told you because she thought Jimmy already did," Ollie said to her mama.

"I may have led that woman to the river, but I did not force her to drink."

"Maybe she wanted to tell," Ollie said. "Like Daddy always says about folks in trouble—how their soul searches for help, even if their mortal body doesn't know it."

"Maybe, though I'm not certain we can do much."

"What do you mean, Mama? We have to do something."

Susanna Love shook her head. "The Good Lord helps those who help themselves. If Virginia refuses to recant her confession and Jimmy keeps with his notion of not knowing anyone his daddy associated with, then I don't see what we can do."

"But there's no need for the list anymore."

"There certainly is. How else can we consider the suspects if we don't have that list of names? We don't know folks 'round these parts. I'm telling you, Ollie, we can offer friendship and warm bread, but I doubt we'll be able to do more than that."

Ollie realized her mama had not come to the same conclusion about Jimmy. "Mama, do you feel better now?" she said.

"I don't see how meeting Virginia would make anyone with a heart beating in their chest feel *better*, but I do understand why we need to stay and do what we can. And I don't think we should mention what she said about the frogs. I'm afraid it would only shame the boy."

"Yes, ma'am."

"That poor child has experienced more than enough shame in his life. He doesn't need us parading it out in public. Do I have your word?"

"I promise," Ollie said.

17

Ellen spent the afternoon flushing Mrs. Mahoney's toilet. She wandered into the bathroom on the main floor off the kitchen and came out hollering, "She's got a flusher! An honest-to-goodness flusher!" Ollie tried explaining that of course they had seen toilets before, but Ellen was only five and couldn't remember a time when they had unlimited access to anything other than their portable outhouse.

Mrs. Mahoney didn't seem to mind Ellen's fascination. "These floors were made for the patter of little feet," she said in response to Ellen's running from room to room and shouting excitement about the lace window curtains and quilted coverlets on the beds upstairs.

"Look at this, Ellen," Ollie said to her baby sister when Mrs. Mahoney was out back showing the reverend where he could park his Chevy truck and trailer. "Do you see this?" Ollie was reaching into Mrs. Mahoney's Frigidaire and showing off the ready-made ice cubes that came in perfect squares.

"Ooooo," Ellen crooned. "It's like you said, Ollie. Real ice and loads of it! Here, give me some." Ellen flicked an empty hand up at her sister.

Ollie quickly shut Mrs. Mahoney's freezer. "Mind your manners. It's not ours to take without asking." She knew Ellen would be asking and hoped the answer was yes.

"She must be rich," Ellen said, swinging her arms out wide and twirling in a circle. Her blue calico dress swirled out from her skinny legs like petunia petals.

"Not really," Ollie said. "Most folks have sinks and toilets. It is 1957, Ellen—even in Binder."

Ellen was undeterred. "Ice and flushers both. I might as well be in heaven."

Ollie couldn't agree more.

Mrs. Mahoney lived in a two-story, four-bedroom house. She used the bedroom on the main floor, so she gave two of the three upstairs rooms to her new guests. Ollie's mama and daddy would sleep with Ellen in one room, and the four other girls took the second bedroom. Ollie noticed the last upstairs bedroom was locked tight, but didn't pay it much mind. Compared to their travel trailer, there was space to spare.

Aside from the bedrooms and bathrooms, there was a kitchen, a library, and a front sitting room. Ollie imagined having a house like Mrs. Mahoney's someday, when she was grown and out on her own. She stood at the kitchen sink, looking out the window over a vegetable garden, and pretended it was all hers. She imagined pulling fresh cold milk from the refrigerator and pouring it into a tall glass for her someone special. A real glass of cold milk was something her mama couldn't offer her daddy. Susanna could only offer a tin mug full of coffee or a tumbler of warm lemonade. Ollie imagined cooking her meals with a simple flick of a switch on the stove top and washing dishes in a sink of hot suds. No more burning the eggs over a campfire or waiting for water to boil. And the bathtub! The thought of closing her day with a hot bubble bath was almost more than Ollie could stand!

"You're certain we're no bother?" Ollie could hear her daddy say as he and Mrs. Mahoney came in the back door.

"Heavens no," Mrs. Mahoney said.

"We're a large brood. We'd be happy to keep to our trailer, if we could use your land."

Ollie's heart sank down into the pit of her stomach. After a few hours of electricity, she couldn't imagine going back to the camping life. She crept quietly over to the kitchen doorway, peeked around the corner, and looked down the hallway.

Mrs. Mahoney was shaking her head. "No, no," she said. "I couldn't bear to think of your precious girls crammed into that thing when I have empty beds inside. Besides, I'm a lonely widow woman. Children's voices will do me good—put life back into these old walls." She gave a soft pat to the gold-flecked wallpaper.

Ollie leaned back into the kitchen and let out a relieved breath.

"We thank you kindly," Reverend Love said. "We will pull our weight. If you don't mind my saying, I've noticed a few areas that could use some attention. I'd like to make a list for the girls to start on first thing tomorrow."

"I suppose I could use some help pulling the vegetable garden into shape, and the trim has needed new paint for years. I've never liked heights."

"Consider it done."

Ollie peeked her head around the corner one more time. She saw Mrs. Mahoney take her daddy's hand and cradle it gently in her time-worn fingers. "You are a good man, Reverend. I don't care what the rest of the town has to say."

Ollie tried to read the expression on her daddy's face. It looked something like worry, and she was sure he was concerned about bringing their family's problems upon such a kind and generous soul as Mrs. Mahoney. Still—ice *and* flushers. Ollie couldn't bring herself to be sorry.

• • •

"What do you suppose she keeps in here?" Camille said that first night at Mrs. Mahoney's. They were standing in the upstairs hallway, outside the locked bedroom.

"Dead children," Martha said flatly.

Ellen was all eyes. "For real?"

"Don't listen to Martha. She's trying to get you riled," Ollie said.

Camille began twisting her nightgown in her hands. "Dead," she said, voice trembling. "Deprived of life, no longer living."

"Now look what you've done!" Ollie said to Martha. "Nice work. Don't worry, Camille. Martha didn't mean dead like that. She meant something else entirely. Didn't you, Martha?"

"Yes, Camille," Martha said. "I meant dead like . . . um . . ." She was searching.

"Lacking energy?" Camille asked, hopeful.

"Right. As in *dead tired*," Ollie assured. "Like we are after this long day. That's all she was saying. Now come on, we're supposed to be brushing our teeth."

It was late, and Susanna Love had ordered her girls upstairs to get ready for bed. They crowded into the bathroom, brushing teeth and spitting the foamy paste into the pink ceramic basin. Ollie stationed herself by the faucet, turning the white handles on and off with each rinse of a sister's toothbrush.

When they were done, Martha walked over to the locked door. "That's odd," she said.

"Mind your business," Ollie warned. "A person is allowed some privacy. Mrs. Mahoney is kind enough to let us stay with her, don't go ruining it by nosing around."

"Ollie's right," Gwen agreed.

"*Ollie's right*," Martha mocked, rolling her eyes. "Looks like a simple lock."

"Martha, don't you dare," Ollie warned.

"Or what? You'll tattle? Then Daddy will think we're causing trouble and make us move on. Is that what you want?"

"Oh, not me," Ellen said. "I ain't even made ice pops in Mrs. Mahoney's Frigidaire freezer yet."

"Mama'll be coming up soon," Ollie said. "You'll get caught."

"She's still got a stack of dishes to wash. We've got a minute or two." Martha reached into her curls and pulled out a black bobby pin. "Perfect." She straightened the pin, slid it into the lock, and gave it two short jabs to the left and one to the right. Then she turned the knob and pushed the door open.

The girls stood frozen.

"You go," Martha said to Camille.

Camille gave a small shake of her head and stepped back.

"Fine, I'll go first."

Martha went, followed by Ellen, then Ollie.

"Lord, save us all," Gwen said, standing at the doorway, watching.

Camille hung back in the shadow of the hallway.

"It's a bunch of baby stuff," Martha said, lifting a tiny blanket on the bassinet and fluffing dust into the air.

The room was a cheery yellow nursery with a sturdy white crib, changing table, rocking chair, and dresser. Over in the corner, above the crib, was a mobile that dangled elephants and giraffes, stars and moons—all hanging from bright yellow strings.

Ollie couldn't imagine a finer place to lay your sweet baby down.

Martha dragged a finger along the thick dust that layered the dresser. "I wonder why she keeps this all locked up. What's the big secret?"

"She's gonna see your mark on that dresser, Martha," Ollie said. "Stop touching things."

Martha wasn't worried. "It's not like she comes in here. How many years has it been since Mrs. Mahoney had a baby?"

Ollie noticed Ellen over by the corner window lifting a beautiful porcelain doll from a small chair. "Put that down," Ollie said. "Come on out. We shouldn't be in here."

"But she's so pretty," Ellen said, tracing her finger along the doll's cheek and down to its chin. "Mrs. Mahoney isn't even playing with her. She's lonely, I know it. She wants to come out of this dark room and play with Baby Doll Sue."

"Absolutely not," Ollie said.

"I'll name her Madelyn," Ellen said, enchanted.

"You'll do no such thing." Ollie knew she sounded like her mother, but didn't care. She pulled the doll out of Ellen's hands and returned it to the miniature chair that sat in the corner of the nursery. "Out," she said, pushing her sisters toward the door. "And no one breathes a word about this room."

The girls tumbled out before Ollie's strong hands and filed into their assigned bedroom.

"That was creepy," Martha said, climbing into the wide bed and taking up more than her share of blankets.

Ollie slid in next to her sister and tugged the covers her way. The clean, flowery smell of the newly washed pillowcase filled her nose. She didn't miss the smell of campfire smoke that usually permeated every stitch of fabric in her life. She didn't miss that smell at all. The last thing she wanted was Martha ruining things for everyone. "It's a nursery, Martha," she said. "Nothing creepy about it."

"Yeah, but why would a two-hundred-year-old woman keep a nursery?" Martha asked. Then she reached down to where Ellen was nestled at the foot of the bed. "Unless she really *does* keep dead children in there," she said, tickling Ellen.

Ellen kicked and giggled and screamed from Martha's tickles until their mama came up the stairs, carted her off to the parents' bed, and turned off the lights.

18

Ollie thought Gwen was the luckiest of all her sisters because, on their second day at Mrs. Mahoney's, she got to celebrate her eleventh birthday. None of the Love sisters had ever celebrated their birthday in a real kitchen, with an oven-baked cake (as opposed to a skillet cake) and blue paper streamers twisting across the ceiling.

"Can I talk to Nana Shirlene first?" Gwen asked.

"Of course," Susanna said.

They were talking about Gwen's birthday present—a phone call to their Nana Shirlene, who was Susanna's mother. She lived in Savannah, and Ollie only got to see her every three or four years when they made it back that way, but they tried to call her on each of the girls' birthdays. On their last trip to Georgia, Nana Shirlene sewed them the yellow and pink patchwork quilt that Ollie now sat on during all of her daddy's sermons. She liked to imagine that Nana was right there with her.

The one downside about Gwen's present was having to use the only pay telephone in Binder. By sorry luck, it happened to sit on the back wall of Carter's Fresh. Of course, Mrs. Mahoney had offered to let the family use her telephone, but Reverend Love wouldn't hear of it. They had taken so much in room and board, he wasn't going to add a long-distance bill to the load. He had the means to pay for it, but it wasn't proper manners to use someone's phone for a toll call, and Reverend Love was nothing if not a Southern gentleman.

Ollie thought the phone call was a fine present—even if it didn't come wrapped in bows. Nana Shirlene was unrefined joy. Her voice bubbled and crackled like a Fourth of July sparkler whenever she spoke to her grand-darlings. That's what she called the girls, her grand-darlings.

Reverend Love came into the kitchen. "We spaghetti?" he asked, grinning.

"Spaghetti ready!" Ellen said as she popped over to her daddy's side.

"And cute as can be," he said down to his littlest one. Ellen beamed. The North Star had nothing on Ellen's smile.

Everlasting and Susanna gathered their girls and went into town. Ollie was feeling nervous about going, but Nana Shirlene would be waiting for the call, and Ollie knew her mama had been looking forward to it for weeks.

When they made it to the store, an old farmer was busying the telephone, so the Love family roamed the aisles while they waited. Ollie was careful not to touch anything and quick to pull Ellen's wandering hands away from the colorful boxes and bags that lined the shelves. Mrs. Carter stood in vigil behind her till and scrutinized their every move. Finally, the man hung up and walked out. Susanna took brisk steps toward the telephone.

"Sorry," Mrs. Carter called out from the front. "Phone's out of order."

"But the gentleman was on it," Susanna protested.

"What gentleman?"

"The farmer, he was using it."

"I ain't seen no farmer," Mrs. Carter said, itching for a good scrap. "It's my telephone and I say it's out of order."

"Dial tone's fine," Reverend Love said as he held the phone to his ear. He was so quick while the ladies were busy arguing, Mrs. Carter didn't even have a chance to speak out. "And it's taking my money without a problem. Oh, listen"—he was having fun making Mrs. Carter into a liar—"it's ringing." He handed Gwen the receiver. "Guess it's not broken after all. What a blessing."

"You're a heap of headaches," Mrs. Carter said, angry fists balled up on her hips.

"S'at right?" Reverend Love asked, taking the tone from the locals.

"No one wants you here. Why don't you pack up and go?"

Ollie watched her daddy choose his words carefully. "You take issue with us helping the Koppels." It wasn't a question.

"They's good-for-nothing thieves."

"Didn't pay their tab?"

"Not a dime. Run it high and ignored it. I had to kick them out completely."

"And you never got paid," he said.

Ollie wondered where her daddy might be going with his line of questioning.

"Like I said, they's thievin' folk. Henry Koppel didn't have a mind to pay his tab—never meant to. Takin' groceries when you know you can't pay is the same as stealin'."

"Made you feel cheated?" Reverend Love asked.

"Course," Esther Carter said, smug as ever.

"Angry, too."

"Mighty angry."

"Enough to want him gone?"

Esther Carter spit a shot of tobacco juice into a coffee can. "I ain't killed nobody."

"But you said he stole from you. I'd say that's a pretty clear motive." Reverend Love pulled a toothpick out of his shirt pocket and pushed it between his teeth.

"You don't scare me, preacher man."

"You should know I wrote the attorney general, Mr. Bruce Atkins, and asked him to come do an investigation. He should be here in a few days."

"Is that true, Daddy?" Ollie asked. "Did you really ask someone to do an investigation?"

"I most certainly did."

Ollie's gut twisted and her heart began skipping inside her chest.

Reverend Love reached back into his shirt pocket and pulled out a book of matches. "By the way," he said, "we found these matches in the Marshalls' field when we were packing up. Funny how they showed up after the fire." He tossed the matchbook onto the counter. It was tattered and charred, with only one match left and a blue ink scroll across the cover that read *Carter's Fresh*. "Do you think one of your boys could have set the fire?" he asked.

Esther Carter started hollering and flinging her arms up toward the ceiling. She called Reverend Love a "good-for-nothing money grubber" and ordered the family out. Gwen had finished talking to Nana Shirlene, which was the most important thing, and Susanna had visited for a couple of minutes before her husband had to shepherd the family out of the market.

"Don't worry," Reverend Love said to his girls. "We'll call her back when we get to another town. She'll understand."

Ollie was sad to miss out on her part of the phone call, but she knew her daddy was right. Nana Shirlene would understand. She always did.

• • •

Jimmy joined the family for Gwen's birthday party. Ollie invited Moody to the party as well, but he refused to come. He did say, however, he wouldn't turn down a piece of chocolate cake if it came knocking. The meal was nothing fancy—ham hock broth with split peas and wax beans. It was from a hog that had been given to them in their last town. Susanna Love possessed a serious talent for stretching food. Simple as it was, it was a meal filled with laughter and the anticipation of chocolate cake. Perfect, really.

"Presents! Presents!" Ellen insisted once the last bit of soup had been ladled out of the pot. She wasn't one for waiting. The youngest of the Love girls stood ceremoniously in front of Gwen and said, "My present is to allow you to sleep with Baby Doll Sue for one whole night." She was overflowing with excitement.

"I can't think of a more perfect gift," Gwen said. "I will cuddle her tightly."

"Not too tight," Ellen said. "She doesn't like to be squished."

"Medium tight, then," Gwen answered.

Ellen grinned and gave a satisfied nod.

Camille handed her sister a walnut shell that had been split open and then tied back together with string. Gwen pulled the string loose and opened the shell to reveal an Indian Head penny. "Oh, Camille," she said. "I love it."

"You can spend it if you want," Camille said.

"No, I'll save it. It's a special penny."

"It *is* special, of unusual quality."

Ollie reminded her that she had already completed an entire day of Gwen's chores, which she thought, after the phone call to Nana Shirlene, was the nicest present of all.

Martha stood before her younger sister, dug around in her pocket a moment, and pulled out a small white rock. "It's a fossil," she said, "from the Mississippi. I found it when we crossed over this last time."

"Really?" Gwen asked, turning the cream-colored stone gently in her hand.

"See the swirls on this side? They're left behind from an ancient water snail."

Gwen tried to fold the stone fossil back into Martha's hand. "I can't take this," she said. "It's too nice."

Martha pulled away. "I want you to have it."

"Thank you, Martha. I couldn't have hoped for a nicer gift."

"It's nothing." Martha shrugged, uncomfortable with the praise.

"Shall we have cake, then?" their mama asked.

"Wait," Jimmy said. "I haven't given my gift."

Ollie couldn't imagine what Jimmy could give Gwen—he hardly had enough to keep his own self going.

"All right, son," Reverend Love said. "Go ahead."

Jimmy walked out onto the porch and came back with a sawed-off milk carton. *Of course,* thought Ollie, *what else?*

"This here is a Southern leopard frog," Jimmy

said, carefully tilting the milk carton for Gwen to see. "They're clever ones. They like water, but'll swim away if you let 'em go." He was squatting down next to Gwen's chair. "See them legs? These fellas are hunted for those beautiful legs. If you ever see frog legs on a menu, they're likely from a leopard frog."

"That's disgusting," Martha moaned. "And it's a pet. They're against the rules." She was referring to the rule their daddy set about how they couldn't keep pets because it wasn't fair to move an animal from town to town. Ollie thought it the most ironic thing, given how he had no problem doing exactly that to his own daughters.

"Well," Reverend Love said, "I'd say it's up to Mrs. Mahoney. This is her home, after all."

Mrs. Mahoney was hovering over the frog, fascinated. "What an interesting creature," she said. "Why don't you keep it on the porch, Gwen?"

"It's best to keep them outside anyway," Jimmy said to Mrs. Mahoney. Then he turned back to Gwen. "He'll eat any bug you can dig up—four times a day. He prefers silkworms or wax worms, but will take a cricket if that's all you got. Make sure they's live bugs, 'cuz a frog won't eat anything that's dead. Keep some wet leaves in his carton and a bit of water; he likes the big maple leaves best 'cuz they don't dry out as easy."

"Thank you." Gwen took the sawed-off milk carton and set it down next to the Indian Head penny.

"And you'll have to let him go come winter. Frogs need to hibernate, you know," Jimmy added. "They can't get a good enough rest in a milk carton. He'll need to burrow down under a lake somewhere if he's to make it through the cold."

"I won't forget," Gwen promised.

"Is it true what you said, Jimmy?" Ellen asked. "Do folks honest-to-goodness eat the legs off these frogs?" She was squatting next to the milk carton and looking down on Gwen's new frog.

"Some do."

"You ever eat frog legs, Jimmy?"

Ollie remembered the story Jimmy's mama told about his daddy tricking him into eating some of his frogs. She exchanged a nervous look with her mama.

"Not on purpose," Jimmy said.

"Me neither," Ellen pronounced.

Susanna dished up slices of cake while Mrs. Mahoney poured everyone an ice-cold glass of milk. "Eat up," Susanna said once everyone was served and she had set aside two slices for Moody and Virginia. Jimmy would deliver both on his way home later that evening.

Ollie wondered what those visits might be like,

with Jimmy on the free side of the bars and Virginia on the other. She imagined how scared Jimmy must be for his mama, but also for himself if he confessed. She wondered if Virginia would even let him confess, or if Sheriff Burton would believe them. Ollie used to think there was a measure of goodness in everyone, but the more she learned about Henry Koppel, the less certain she was. He had hurt his little family beyond belief.

Ollie let the full chocolate flavor of Gwen's birthday cake fill her mouth and soothe her troubled spirit.

"Well, Mrs. Love," the reverend said to his wife once his plate was licked clean, "you've gone and done it again. I do believe that was the best cake I've ever tasted."

"Absolutely," Mrs. Mahoney agreed.

"It was nothing but a box of Duncan Hines," Ollie's mama said.

"It was wonderful," Ollie said. "What do you think, Jimmy? Wasn't that one of the best cakes you've ever tasted?"

Jimmy flushed. He dropped his head and said, "The only cake."

"That can't be right," Ollie said. "You've had cake before."

"No, I ain't." It was clear the boy was uncomfortable.

"But what about on your birthday?" Ellen piped in. "Or Christmas? Or your mama's birthday?"

Reverend Love scooped his youngest girl up into his arms, sending her into a fit of giggles and causing her to stop the cake interrogation. The other four Love girls sat dumbfounded—jaws gaping in disbelief. They knew poor, but couldn't imagine living a whole life without a stitch of cake. How does that happen to a person?

"When is your birthday, son?" Susanna asked.

"January twenty-seventh, but we were never much for celebratin'," Jimmy answered.

"That's fine," Susanna said. "But as long as there is breath in my lungs, you will have cake on your birthday. That's what the American post office is for. Now, what kind do you prefer?"

"You're silly, Mama," Ellen said. "If he ain't never had cake, how can he know what he likes best?"

"Excellent point," Susanna said. "I shall make and send you a different kind every year until you can choose a favorite."

Jimmy smiled.

"Look at that," Ellen said. "His smile is bigger than his whole face!"

19

Ollie spent the next morning cleaning clumped leaves out of Mrs. Mahoney's rain gutters and pulling weeds from her brick walkway. Ollie's daddy was determined to turn his family's stay into a blessing. Not that Ollie minded the work. She loved Mrs. Mahoney like a bee loves a fat flower. If it weren't for her, Ollie knew they'd be back in the travel trailer, two states over by now.

After her chores were done, Ollie asked her mama if she could go for a walk. She was hoping to find Jimmy and spend some alone time with him. Her mama agreed to let her go for a short time, and Ollie found Jimmy thigh deep in Rutger's Marsh, the one located at the base of Mason's Holler.

"Hey, Jimmy," she hollered from across the bog.

"Hisht!" Jimmy whispered. The sharp sound sent

frogs leaping away in all directions. "Da'gum it, Ollie! Now look what you done. Took me an hour to get this close."

"Sorry," Ollie squeaked.

"Them's Cope's frogs, too. They're tiny buggers and harder to catch than most."

"I'll leave if you want to try again."

"Nah," he said. "Forget it." He stepped out of the marsh. Green moss clung to his legs, and black swampy mud covered his feet.

"You gonna clean that off?"

"Clean what off?"

"That stinky scum you've got hanging from your bony hide."

Jimmy could have been angry, but he wasn't. "You are a trial and a tribulation, Olivene Love. A trial and a tribulation."

"You've been hanging around my daddy too much. You're starting to sound like a preacher."

"S'at so awful?"

Ollie laughed. "Man alive, would he love to hear you say that." Then she shaded her eyes from the bright sun and asked, "You fixin' to be a preacher, Jimmy Koppel?"

"No way," he said. "I just think some of the words

are pretty. I couldn't do what you do, Ollie. I couldn't leave my home and ramble around lookin' for souls to save."

"I'm not looking for any souls to save. That's my daddy's job."

"Well, I don't want to leave here. My mama, my frogs . . . they need me too much."

"But you'll have to go once they send your mama away, right?" Ollie asked, already knowing the answer.

"If Sheriff Burton has his way, I will."

"What will happen to your frogs?"

Jimmy shook his head. "I can't think about that. I gotta keep hope that I'll find a way to get my mama free." Then he grinned that extra-wide smile of his. "So you think I stink, do you?"

"Like rotten fish."

"And the mud on my toes is disgusting?"

"Completely."

Jimmy nodded slowly and walked over to Ollie. When he came to her side, he lifted her up by her shoulders and tossed her into the middle of that filthy bog.

"Jimmy Koppel!" Ollie hollered between gasps and laughs. "My mama will have your neck!" She was head to toe in the muck of it all.

Jimmy clasped his hands like an angel and said, ever so sweetly, "Why, whatever are you talking about, Mrs. Love? Throw Ollie in the marsh? Heavens no! I ain't even seen her today."

Ollie pulled herself out of Rutger's Marsh. She was dripping with strings of moss and black mud flecks.

"Looks like you've got a passenger," Jimmy said, pointing to her skirt pocket.

Ollie looked down and saw her dress twitching. She reached into her pocket and pulled out a green-gray Cope's frog. As quick as she opened her hand, the frog leapt out and down into the marsh. "Gracious Lord!" Ollie said.

"There she goes, swearing again."

"That's hardly swearing."

"It counts."

"All right, Reverend Jimmy, I guess you caught me."

"Come on," Jimmy said. "Let's go to Moody's. He has a hose."

Ollie followed her friend up the holler to Moody's house.

The old man met them at his door, ran his eyes from Ollie's soggy hair all the way down to her wet feet and said, "Leave any water for the fish?"

"He threw me into Rutger's Marsh," Ollie said, pointing a thumb to Jimmy.

Jimmy smiled. "Let's call it a playful toss."

Moody lifted his chin. "Let's call it smelly."

"We were hoping to use your hose," Ollie said.

Moody went back into his house and returned with a chunk of pink soap. "Jimmy knows where it is," he said with a nod off to the left.

Ollie scrubbed over her dress and then handed the soap to Jimmy.

"All right," he said. "I'll take the hint." He took his shirt off and scrubbed.

Ollie spread out on a patch of clover that was growing in the sunshine. The warm afternoon rays seeped into her skin and made her feel woozy with relaxation. Jimmy stretched out next to her. "Aahh," he said. "Nothing better than this."

"Not a blessed thing," Ollie agreed. She kept her face to the brilliant sky and took the moment to say what she needed to. "My daddy's called for the attorney general to come over from Little Rock."

"I heard."

"He'll do an investigation to find out who killed your pa." Her words were heavy with the implication.

"Guess so."

"Does that worry you?" Ollie had to ask.

"Why should I worry?" Jimmy asked.

Ollie was quiet and let the words sift through her mind—trying to come up with the perfect ones. "Well," she said, "what if they free your mama, but then put the person who *did* kill him in prison? What then?"

"I suppose they'd have to do that."

"I couldn't stand to think of you in jail, Jimmy." Ollie's words rushed out like water from a fire hydrant. "What's the good getting your mama out of jail if they're only going to put you in her place? I wish my daddy never wrote to that Bruce Atkins. I wish we could have found a way to bust your mama free and have both of you come away with us. I don't fault you. Your daddy was a terrible man, and you were only protecting your mama."

Jimmy sat up. "What are you saying?"

"The attorney general," she said. "Daddy said we only had to prove it wasn't your mama who killed your pa. But if the attorney general is coming all this way, he's not going to just find out who *didn't* do it. He'll do his investigation and—"

"Ollie. I didn't kill my pa."

The words sucked the living breath out of her lungs. "But your mama said he was beating on her and she passed out."

"That's true."

"And she told us about the awful trick of cooking up your frogs and how angry you were."

Jimmy's words came out like sharp jabs. "I didn't kill him."

Ollie realized she was shaking and wrapped her arms around her body. "You didn't?"

"Do you think I'm a murderer?"

"Not a murderer," she said. "Just saving your mama."

"I can't believe you! You're no better than everyone else in this stinkin' town! How could you think I could do such a thing? Because I'm a Koppel, that makes me capable of murdering my own pa? Holy Moses, listen to yourself!"

"I'm sorry, Jimmy. I just—"

"Leave me alone." His words cut Ollie to the core. "I wish you'd never come to Binder—you and your whole stupid family. Go back to preaching and leave me alone!" He stood up and took off down the path. Ollie jumped up and ran after him.

"Stop," she called, grabbing his hand and yanking him to a halt. "You're right. It was a horrible thing to say. Don't be mad, please."

Jimmy turned his eyes high and low, left and

right—anywhere but to Ollie's pleading face. She held tight to his hand. "Please," she said again. "Don't leave it like this."

Finally, he looked at Ollie. "I didn't do it."

"I know," she said. "You couldn't. I know that now. I was mixed up. Your mama told us how he was so terrible to you, making you eat your frogs. I got confused, is all."

He slit his eyes and looked real deep into hers. "I was mad at him, that's certain. He was sittin' in my mama's rocker, sucking on a leg bone and laughin' at me. Thought he was so funny. He started making *rib-bit* noises and sayin' how I et up five of my best ones. I could have killed him right then and there, but I didn't. I ran off to be by myself so I wouldn't do something stupid. I didn't want to bring trouble to my ma."

"I'm sorry. Can we forget I said anything and go back to being friends?"

Jimmy placed his other hand over hers. "I'm glad you came today."

"Me, too."

Jimmy's lip curled into a half smile. "Someday I'll teach you how to catch a Cope's frog the right way."

Ollie laughed. "I've had enough of your fishing

lessons, thank you very much." Then she turned and headed down the holler. "And put your shirt back on, why don't you?" she said over her shoulder. "Remember, I'm a lady."

"If'n you call twelve a lady," Jimmy said, full of chuckles.

"You're a regular comedian, Jimmy Koppel. Downright hilarious."

20

Two days later, Jimmy stood on Mrs. Mahoney's threshold with a cluster of poppies, daisies, and hollyhocks in his hand.

"Look who's all shiny and new," Martha said.

"Never mind her, Jimmy," Ollie said, coming to the door. She hardly recognized her friend. His hair was clean and combed, his skin polished. He was wearing a button-down plaid shirt that was three sizes too big and a tie that hung down too low, but he looked nice. Handsome, almost. He was even wearing shoes—with laces! "Where's the party?" Ollie asked.

"No party," Jimmy said. "I guess I'm tired of offending the *lady*."

"Very funny," Ollie said, reaching for the flowers.

"They ain't for you." Jimmy pulled the bunch of huddled blossoms back slightly. "They're for Mrs. Mahoney."

"Oh," Ollie said, surprised at the disappointment she felt.

Jimmy laughed. "You're a goof. I just thought Mrs. Mahoney might like some flowers. Where is she?"

Ollie pointed to the kitchen and followed Jimmy. Mrs. Mahoney smiled when he handed her the flowers and fairly danced over to a cupboard to pull out a vase.

"I can't recall the last time a gentleman brought me flowers." She was glowing. "Now, where shall I set these?" Her twilight blue eyes scanned the room. Susanna Love had rolled noodles for chicken soup earlier in the day and left them drying across the kitchen table. Camille and Gwen were using the coffee table for a game of checkers, and Martha had her map and travel books spread out on the library desk. With seven new boarders, table space was at a premium. Ollie opened her mouth to apologize, but stopped when she realized Mrs. Mahoney did not seem the least bit upset. That woman stood in the middle of her kitchen, clutching her cut-glass vase of wildflowers, and soaked up the fresh life buzzing around her. "This spot will do," she said, pushing aside a few strips of noodles on the kitchen table. "Perfect."

Jimmy looked at Ollie. "I've got a surprise. Can you get away for a while?"

"I wanna go, too." It was Ellen, standing in the kitchen doorway.

Ollie's expression fell flat. "He didn't invite you."

"How come I can't go?" Ellen asked.

Susanna stepped into the kitchen at that moment with a basket of plums in her hands.

"Mama," Ellen whined, "Ollie won't let me go to the Jimmy-surprise."

Susanna looked at Jimmy with his tie and laced shoes and buttoned-up collar. Then she turned to Ollie. "Take your baby sister," she said.

"But, Mama—" Ollie began.

"It's fine," Jimmy said. "Ellen's welcome."

Jimmy led the way out toward Rutger's Marsh. Ollie looked down the street and noticed the steeple on the abandoned church poking out over the rooftops. "What's with that old church?" she asked.

Jimmy shrugged. "I don't know," he said. "Been closed up my whole life."

"Do you know why?"

"Nope."

"How could you not know?" Ollie pressed. "I thought everyone knew everything that ever happened in this town."

"I know it's a nice day for a picnic," he said, flashing his smile and slipping one hand into Ollie's and the other into Ellen's.

When they got over to the mossy side of the marsh, Ollie saw two burlap sacks with another bunch of wildflowers propped inside an empty soda bottle. She couldn't imagine a more beautiful sight.

"It's nothing but peanut butter on wheat bread," Jimmy said.

"I love peanut butter," Ellen said, sitting down on one of the sacks.

Ollie sighed and sat down next to her sister.

"Hey, Jimmy," Ellen said, "you look real nice today."

Jimmy tugged at his bagging shirtsleeves. "This was my daddy's."

"And the tie, too?" Ellen asked.

"Yeah." He let out a short laugh. "Not that he wore it much. He wasn't one for fancy things. It's a mite big, I reckon, but I think it looks all right. Moody helped me with the sandwiches and lent me his shoes. He's got smaller feet, so it took some work to get 'em on."

"So handsome," Ellen said with an approving nod.

"Think so?" Jimmy had that twinkle about him again.

The whip-poor-wills called over the treetops, and the sun filtered through the branches, crafting mottled light across their picnic area.

"Sure do," Ellen said.

Jimmy leaned in and whispered, "What about your big sister here? Do you think she agrees?"

Ellen looked over to Ollie. "Nah," she said. "She thinks you're too skinny."

"Ellen!" Ollie gasped.

Jimmy fell back, laughing.

"I never said that," Ollie said.

"It's okay." Jimmy was still laughing. "I'm just teasing."

"Hey, Ellen," Ollie said. "Why don't you go pull some dandelions from that field, and we'll show Jimmy how to make one of those necklaces."

"Really?" Ellen asked.

"Sure, just stay close where I can see you."

Ellen stood up. "You're gonna love them, Jimmy. They're the prettiest things." Then she turned to Ollie. "Don't eat my half of the sandwich."

Ollie ran a finger across her chest. "Cross my heart."

Ellen skipped farther into the field to gather dandelions.

"I've always loved hollyhocks," Ollie said, pulling a blossom from the soda-bottle vase. "See? When you turn one upside down, it looks like a dancing lady." The round petals of the pink flower flitted in the breeze like a delicate ball gown. "When I get my own house, I'm going to plant a whole bushel of hollyhocks along the east wall. That's where they grow best, with their faces toward the morning sun."

"You ain't going to stick to the road, like your daddy?"

"Heck, no. I know my daddy was born for preaching, but it's not for me."

"Are you a believer, Ollie?"

"I think so," Ollie said, slowly. "I know my daddy believes in his work. He loves people and loves the Lord and just wants to get the two together. It's not the message I have a problem with, it's the traveling." Ollie leaned back and closed her eyes, imagining the life ahead of her. "I want to live in a real house with a mailbox and garden rows. I want a claw-foot bathtub and my very own washer and dryer. I want my children to go to a regular school with a real teacher. I don't understand why my daddy can't find a church and settle down."

"Have you ever told your daddy?"

Ollie didn't want to talk about the preaching road anymore. "Tell me what you want, Jimmy."

"What I want?"

"Sure," she said. "Tell me your dreams."

Jimmy was quiet for the longest time. He opened up his sandwich and fiddled with the wax paper it had been wrapped in. "I s'pose I don't rightly know," he said. "Bringing my mama home, I guess."

"That goes without saying, but there's got to be more. This life you're living can't be all you want. You're lost in this town."

Jimmy leaned back on one elbow. "Let me tell you somethin', Miss Olivene Love. When I was a small guy, maybe 'bout Ellen's age, I wandered off, away from my house. I was lookin' for frogs, but had never been very far by myself before. I headed out south, down by the river."

"The river where your daddy was found?"

"Yeah. It runs down the holler and into this marsh here." Jimmy shuddered and went on. "Anyway, I ended up stuck—deep in a thicket of hawthorn bushes. Everywhere I turned, there was another thorny bush cuttin' me. I had blood runnin' down my arms and legs and no idea where I was. The more I tried to move, the thicker the clump of hawthorns seemed to get. I could barely see the sky."

"Lost," Ollie said, understanding.

"No. That's just it. I wasn't lost. I had no idea where I was—I couldn't see my way out, but I was right there in my own backyard. I was only twenty yards from the back door the whole time. That's how it is sometimes. I may seem lost, but I'm really not. I'll find my way out of this tangle, like I did back then. It may be a mess of thorns, but it's home."

Ollie rested her chin on her knees. "That's the best thing I ever heard."

"That's what I like about you," Jimmy said. "You're easy to be with."

Just then, Ellen came back and dropped an armful of dandelions into Ollie's lap. "Don't smash 'em," she said.

"I wouldn't think of it," Ollie answered.

Ellen sat down and led Jimmy through the steps of linking the flower stems into a chain. "And whatever you do," she said, "you can't put it in your pocket. You have to wear it or hang it up on a nail. I know these things 'cuz I'm five."

"Okay, since you know so much, maybe you can answer a question for me." Jimmy looked serious. "It's very important."

"Go ahead," Ellen said, proud.

"Can I take these dang shoes off? They're killin' my feet."

Ellen giggled as Jimmy pulled on the laces and tugged off the shoes.

"Honest to Pete, them shoes is like coffins!" He yanked off his socks and pushed his crooked toes through the soft tufts of moss. "There you go, little buddies," he said. "Breathe deep."

• • •

Chores were waiting when Ollie and Ellen returned from their picnic with Jimmy. Ellen went inside to help their mama, and Ollie headed around to the backyard. Her daddy had assigned her the ominous task of whipping Mrs. Mahoney's vegetable garden into shape.

"Nice to have you join us," Martha said from her perch on the ladder. She and Camille were helping repaint the house trim. There was green paint streaming down her arm and spotted across her shirt. "Must be nice to laze around in the middle of the day."

"I'll get my work done and you'll get your work done," Ollie said. "Why do you care how I spend my free time?"

Martha teased, "Ollie and Jimmy sittin' in a tree, k-i-s-s-i-n-g."

Camille, who was the official paint dipper, jumped in with "h-i-j-k-l-m-n-o-p . . ."

"That's not how the song goes!" Martha said.

"It's not?" Camille asked.

Martha went on. "Jimmy's been slobbering all over you like a newborn calf. I'm only surprised Daddy allows it."

"We're friends, Martha. That's all."

"And I'm the Queen of England."

Camille, confused, said, "But you're not a queen. You're plain old Martha."

Martha rolled her eyes, and Ollie turned to the vegetable garden box that sat in the far corner of the yard. Mrs. Mahoney had simply tossed handfuls of seeds onto the dark spring soil and prayed good plants would eventually rise up over the weeds. That being her method, tomato plants grew next to strawberries that grew next to bell peppers that grew next to a single cornstalk—all jumbled and mixed in with an amazing selection of thistles and nettles. Oh, the nettles! Ollie had never seen them so tall or so broad. And she knew from sorry experience that there is no safe way to pull a nettle. They have to be shoveled out of the ground. So she went into the shed that sat on the northeast corner of Mrs. Mahoney's yard in search of a shovel.

What she found instead was a pile of Pure Pak milk cartons, washed clean and stacked high. *What would Mrs. Mahoney be doing with a collection of milk cartons?* Ollie asked herself, but as she considered the question, she knew the answer. Of course it had been Mrs. Mahoney sneaking the cartons and cans of food up to Jimmy's place. Who else would do something so neighborly? Ollie may have loved Mrs. Mahoney before, but words could not properly express the swell of emotion that filled her soul at that moment. She pulled a shovel from the shed and turned back to the garden box. Mrs. Mahoney would have the best-looking vegetable patch in all of Binder. No, in all of Arkansas.

21

It took another week before the attorney general got around to showing his face in Binder. He drove up in a 1956 Chrysler Imperial. Ollie recognized it right away. It was exactly like the pictures she saw in magazines, excepting the two American flags fixed to the front bumper. Like freedom blowing wild, that's what he looked like pulling up Main Street.

Of course, Ollie didn't know he was coming that day. She was lucky to catch sight of the car on her way back from taking biscuits to Virginia. There she was, on the steps of Sheriff Burton's office, when that navy blue freedom vehicle rolled up the road and came to a stop in front of her. She knew who was inside without having to ask a single soul. It was Mr. Bruce Atkins, attorney general of the great state of Arkansas, coming to free Virginia Koppel and set the town back on the straight and narrow. It was the answer to all of their prayers, and, Lord, it was a fine sight.

She put on a warm, welcoming smile and began humming "Let My People Go." Her daddy's voice was rich in her head.

"When Israel was in Egypt's land,
  Let my people go!
  Oppressed so hard they could not stand,
  Let my people go!"

"How do, little lady?" Mr. Atkins said as he stepped out of his car. He was wide as he was tall and dressed in the most ridiculous white suit Ollie had ever seen. He wore a cream-colored Stetson and soot black boots that shone brighter than the Hope diamond. For a state official, Ollie thought he was a mite flashy.

"It's a pleasure to meet you," Ollie said with an outstretched hand. "I am Olivene Love, oldest daughter of the Reverend Everlasting Love."

"Ah, the preacher's girl," Mr. Atkins said. The tangy smell of Juicy Fruit gum emanated from his every pore.

"It was my father who sent for you."

Mr. Atkins opened his mouth and shook a bit,

like he was laughing, only no sound came out. "Oh, I'm not sent for by anyone, except maybe the missus," he said. "I was headed out this way, and thought I'd stop in and see what all the commotion was about."

"Yes, sir," Ollie said. "Would you like me to show you to my father? He'd be happy to talk to you—"

"Now hold on to your lacy britches. Let me say how-do to my good friend Tommy."

"Good friend?" Ollie felt sick.

"Sure, I've known Tommy Burton going on twenty-five years. We had our police training together back in the day."

Ollie's legs wobbled. "Twenty-five years?" The promise of those waving flags vanished like cockroaches in the morning light.

"Thereabouts," Mr. Atkins said.

Ollie stayed on the steps while Mr. Atkins went into Sheriff Burton's office. She slipped around the side of the building and listened under an open window as the old friends slapped each other on the back and talked about old times.

Poor Virginia Koppel, Ollie thought. Poor, poor Virginia.

• • •

Ellen was sitting on the roof of Mrs. Mahoney's garage, eating plums off the tree that laid its heavy branches across the tar shingles, when Ollie returned from Sheriff Burton's office.

"Whatcha doin' up there?" Ollie asked.

"Eatin' plums." Purple-pink juice dribbled down Ellen's chin, and slobbered plum pits sat in a slanted pile at her side.

Ollie squinted her eyes against the evening sun. "Does Mama know where you are?"

"I ain't stealing. Mrs. Mahoney said I could eat some of the plums off'n her tree."

"But does Mama know you're up on the roof of that garage?"

Ellen shrugged one shoulder and kept her focus on the half-chewed plum in her hand. Ollie walked around the garage and started up the ladder that was propped against the back wall. When she got to the top rung, she motioned for her baby sister.

"Come on down," she said. "Mama would skin you alive if she saw you up here."

"No she wouldn't," Ellen said.

"Well then, Daddy will."

Reverend Love wasn't one to jump to discipline, but he wasn't afraid of it either. Ellen knew the facts, but didn't move.

"It's pretty up here," she said. "And these plums are the best. The ones down there are all hard and green." She crinkled her nose on "hard and green."

Ollie climbed onto the rooftop and inched over toward Ellen. She was taken by the view—how different it was from the view below—how a few feet up can make the whole world seem new. "It is pretty," she said.

Ellen turned to a pink, blanketed bundle at her side and lifted the fabric to reveal two baby dolls. "Look what else Mrs. Mahoney said I could have."

Nestled next to Baby Doll Sue was the porcelain doll that Ellen had taken a shine to in the locked nursery. Ollie frowned. "What did you do?"

"Nothin'."

"You had to do something. Spill it, or else."

"I ain't scared of you, Ollie. I kept my promise 'bout that room. It was Gwen who told. And since the secret was told, I figured I could invite Madelyn out on a picnic with Baby Doll Sue."

"Gwen," Ollie mumbled. "I should have known."

"Gwen said it was a sin what we did, spyin' in that room. She said her conscience was weighing heavy on her, and she wouldn't be a party with it."

"*To* it, Ellen. She wouldn't be a party *to* it."

"I don't care. Mrs. Mahoney said I could keep

Madelyn forever and ever and that I never have to give her back."

"Was she mad?"

"Nah," Ellen said. "She even said we didn't have to tell Daddy." Then Ellen rested her chin on her knees and let out a soft sigh. "I love Mrs. Mahoney."

"Me, too," Ollie said. "Hey, did she say why she kept a nursery?"

"She looked real sad, but didn't say nothin'."

A voice boomed from below. "Looks like Mrs. Mahoney's got a couple of robins nesting on her roof."

It was Jimmy.

"Come on up," Ellen said as she pulled another plum from a branch.

Jimmy didn't need to be asked twice. He was up the ladder and standing over the girls before Ellen took her first bite into that delicious plum.

"Sit down," Ollie said, nervous at seeing him standing on the slanted roof.

He shuffled a dance and then bent his knees, pretending to be getting a jump ready.

"Knock it off, will you?" Ollie said. "You're going to get us in trouble."

"What for?" Jimmy asked.

"Being on the roof. If Martha sees, she'll run tattling quick as sand."

"Yeah," Ellen piped with a mouthful of plum. "Quick as sand."

Jimmy pointed to the mound of pits at Ellen's side. "Did you eat all of those?"

"Yup," Ellen said, proud of her accomplishment.

"Do you know what plums will do to you?" Jimmy asked.

Ellen's eyes lit up. "Oh I know! I know!" Then she pressed her lips together. "What will they do?"

"Let's just say you'll be glad Mrs. Mahoney has flushers."

"Aw!" Ellen moaned. "Why didn't you tell me, Ollie?"

"I didn't make you eat all those plums," Ollie said.

Ellen scrambled down the ladder and went bawling for Mama. Jimmy laughed and sat down next to Ollie on the garage roof.

"Jimmy, do you know why Mrs. Mahoney would keep a nursery?" She lifted the two dolls Ellen left behind and readjusted the pink blanket around their faces.

"Probably on account of the babies."

"What babies?"

"The ones that died. I've seen a bunch of head-stones, all in a row, over at the cemetery."

"How many?"

"Five. One big one for her husband and four small ones for the babies. According to the dates, they only lived a day or two."

"That's so sad," Ollie said.

"I guess, but it was years ago."

"Still."

"Hey," Jimmy said, "I saw some state car out in front of the jail." There was a definite ring of hope in his words.

"Yeah, but it turns out the attorney general is an old friend of Sheriff Burton. They're likely eating supper and going through old photo albums this very minute."

Jimmy was picking at the tar shingles. "Koppel luck strikes again."

"I've been thinking about that," Ollie said. "Why are we waiting for my daddy or Mr. Atkins to solve this murder? Can't we make our own luck? Can't we figure this out ourselves?"

Jimmy looked uncertain.

"It's like you said about the hawthorn bushes. You didn't stand in the middle of that mess and cry for someone to get you out. You found the way yourself.

It's the same with this. Think about it, Jimmy. You know the people around these parts as much as anyone, right? You ought to know who had it in for your daddy. If you won't make that list of names for my daddy, won't you at least make one for me?"

Jimmy had the most serious face. "Ollie, you ever think about the fact that there is a real murderer wandering 'round? Maybe he doesn't *want* to be found. Maybe he'd do something terrible if we started diggin'."

"Is that why you wouldn't give us any names? You're worried about our safety?"

"I couldn't bear it if you or anyone in your family got hurt. My pa was a big man, a good fighter, and he got his brains bashed out. What do you think that person would do to you, or someone like Ellen?"

"We can take care of ourselves. I know we can figure this out."

"I don't know. Maybe."

"Will you promise to think about it?"

"Okay, Ollie. I'll think about it, for you."

That last part felt good to hear. "It sure is pretty up here," she said, looking out across the dimming sky.

The two friends sat shoulder to shoulder and let the shadows of evening settle over them.

22

Mr. Bruce Atkins spent more time eating pie and sipping juleps than doing any actual investigating. He did manage to grant Virginia about three minutes—long enough to hear her bloody recounting of the skillet incident. Then he sauntered over to Mrs. Mahoney's and scribbled on a yellow legal pad while Reverend and Susanna Love pointed out issues with evidence, or lack thereof. Ollie would have bet her right arm that man wasn't writing anything but doodles on his pad.

His visit was quick as a Jesse James bullet, and Virginia was not any closer to freedom on the day he left. So much for an independent investigation.

Reverend Love was disappointed at the turn of events, but said it could have been expected. He told his family they'd stay a few more days—a week at most—but then they'd be moving on.

Ollie knew there was no arguing with her daddy. The best she could do was spend as much time with Jimmy as her parents would allow. That turned out to be easier said than done, because her daddy kept noticing things like broken tiles in the bathroom and splintered floorboards in the hallway. Ollie's chore list was getting to be longer than the road to Damascus.

"I'm sorry for the mess, dear," Mrs. Mahoney said when Ollie was busy sweeping out the shed at the back of the yard. She gestured to the Pure Pak milk cartons piled on the grass. "That Burton boy used to come around and collect these from me. Said they were used to help the needy. He'd take my old milk cartons and Mary Knuttal's scrap fabric, along with whatever cans of beans or soup he could gather. But he hasn't been by for a while, so I guess we can throw these out."

"Ray Burton?"

"Such a nice young man." She lifted an empty carton in one hand. "Not sure who he was giving them to, or why anyone would need my old milk cartons, but Ray insisted they were being put to good use."

"He gave them to Jimmy," Ollie said, mostly to herself. "Ray is the one who kept bringing those things to the Koppels."

Mrs. Mahoney's eyes brightened. "Wonderful!

Maybe you can tell Jimmy to stop by and pick these up. It's a shame to waste them, if he has need."

"Why would Ray sneak stuff up to the Koppels?"

"It doesn't surprise me he would try to help that poor family. He's a good boy."

Ollie remembered Virginia saying Ray brought her food when his daddy wasn't looking. *Christian character*, she had called it.

Ollie summoned her courage and said, "I've been meaning to apologize about looking in your nursery upstairs on the first night we came. It was wrong of us to go into that room."

Mrs. Mahoney clicked her tongue. "That nursery is a silly thing to keep; a woman my age should know when to let the past be."

"I'm sorry you lost all those babies. It must have been difficult."

Mrs. Mahoney shook her head. "I spent many years longing for children, and then the Good Lord brought your family into my home. My prayers have been answered, after all."

"I'll be sad to leave. You've been so kind."

"I'm hoping you don't leave too soon."

"Daddy says there's not much more we can do here. Not since Mr. Atkins closed the investigation for good."

Mrs. Mahoney's eyes twinkled. "But you'd like to stay, wouldn't you, Ollie?"

Ollie couldn't bring herself to wish it. It hurt too much. But Mrs. Mahoney was standing there, blue eyes dancing, curious. She deserved an honest answer. "Yes," Ollie said.

"Well, maybe this old woman can be of some help." Mrs. Mahoney reached into her skirt pocket and pulled out a brass key. "It's to the church," she said.

"The Lutheran church?"

"It doesn't have to stay Lutheran. It can be anything you want. It was my family who donated the land, so when it closed down, the property came back to me."

Ollie's heart hovered in her chest. "He'll never take it."

"I have already spoken to your father regarding this offer. No journey is more worthy than another, child. His desire to go would not mean he doesn't love you, and your request to stay does not mean you don't appreciate him. There is no right or wrong here, just a family trying to find their way. Go to him. Tell him what you want, and hear what he has to say."

• • •

Ollie's legs were quaking as she stepped into Mrs. Mahoney's library, where her mama and daddy were reading together. They were sharing her mama's Bible on the flowered couch.

She couldn't think of a single word to say, so she stepped in front of them and raised the key in her hand.

"I see Mrs. Mahoney has spoken to you," her daddy said, pulling off his reading glasses. "She said something about an empty church needing a preacher. I told her I wasn't interested, but your mama here convinced me to give it some thought."

Susanna looked at her daughter with a bright and beaming smile.

"What are you saying, Daddy?"

"I'm saying we need to have a family council, and if your sisters agree, we'll consider staying here in Binder for one year."

Her mama reached out and took her daughter's hand. "We understand you want the experience of staying put in a town. You're growing so quickly, and this opportunity may not come our way again. We see how much this means to you."

Ten minutes later, the Love family was sitting around Mrs. Mahoney's Formica table, sweet Ellen on Gwen's lap. They were having a discussion on whether or not to take Mrs. Mahoney up on her offer and stay.

"Typical," Martha said. "Ollie always gets what she wants."

"That's enough," Susanna said.

"And, of course, my opinion means nothing," Martha continued. "Or Daddy's."

"I voted to stay," Reverend Love said.

"Because of Ollie. Not because of what you want."

"I don't mind staying," Gwen said. "It's so important to Ollie. I think it is the right choice."

"Right as in good, just, and proper?" Camille asked. "Or the opposite of left? Or a straight line?"

Gwen reached out to Camille. "The first one," she said.

"Then I choose to stay," Camille said.

Ellen gave a hug to both of her baby dolls. "I want to stay with Mrs. Mahoney forever and ever."

"Then it's settled," Reverend Love said. "We'll give it a year."

Ollie felt an overwhelming sensation of elation mixed with delight and topped off with a dollop of bliss. A giggle came from deep inside and fizzled up through her very soul. "Thank you," she said, wrapping one arm around each parent. "Thank you for listening."

23

It was Ollie who took charge of renovating and cleaning the old church. She climbed the double-tall ladder up to the pine rafters and cleared out cobwebs and dust. To say it was hot at the top of that ladder would not be anywhere near the truth. Sweltering, maybe. Or infernal. Even so, Ollie didn't complain. She swiped spiderwebs as big as Mrs. Mahoney's refrigerator without flinching. She scrubbed the gummed-up dirt on the floor and oiled every square inch of each pew. She soaped and rinsed the windows until they shone clear as the sky itself.

She wasn't alone. Jimmy helped as much as he could—when he wasn't visiting his mama in jail or taking care of his frogs—and her family gave a hand in their spare time. Mrs. Mahoney never let her go an afternoon without bringing in iced lemonade and sun tea.

Ollie also planned a painting party and invited everyone in town—even the Burtons and Mrs. Carter, who sputtered out a laugh at the notion, like her attending would be the most ridiculous thing in the world. But others did come. Lots of them. Reopening that church was breathing new life into all of Binder. Giving folks a reason to pull together.

On the Saturday before the first service—nine short days after Mrs. Mahoney slid that brass key into Ollie's hand—the girl stood under the old tupelo tree, looking at what had become of that church building, when Jimmy walked up to her side.

"You're gonna take root if you stand here long enough," he said.

"That's the idea."

"Welcome to Binder, Olivene Love."

"Thank you, Jimmy Koppel." Ollie looked around. "It's not perfect, but it's pretty close."

"Is Mrs. Mahoney gonna let your family stay on at her place?"

"Until we can gather enough collections to rent our own. She seems to like the company. You know, Jimmy, we haven't forgotten your mama," Ollie said. "I know we've been busy getting the church ready for services tomorrow, but we're not giving up on her. In fact, now that we don't have to worry about my daddy pulling up stakes, we can get down to business."

Jimmy slid his hands into his pockets. "There's no business, Ollie. You know that. Investigation's closed. And with your daddy coming on here"—he nodded toward the church—"he's gonna have to let it go."

"Why?"

"Think about it. How you gonna get a congregation if he keeps makin' everyone angry? How you ever gonna get that home of your own?"

The thought gave Ollie pause. She knew there was some truth in what Jimmy was saying. As the town preacher, holding services in the only church for twenty miles around, Reverend Love might have to ease up on his involvement in town politics. He might have to leave well enough alone.

"Well," Ollie said, "I'm not the town preacher, and nothing is going to stop me from finding a way to get your mama out of jail and keep you in Binder." But as she said the words, doubt slipped under her skin.

"Nine o'clock?" Jimmy said, referring to services the next morning.

"Nine o'clock."

• • •

Susanna Love baked pies, sixteen of them. She and Mrs. Mahoney stayed up late rolling dough and making chopped salads, deviled eggs, noodles and gravy . . . all for the luncheon after the first grand opening of Love's Church.

That was Ollie's vote for the new church name. Her sisters also came up with Friendship Worship, All's Welcome, and Love Abides.

Her daddy didn't like any of them. He removed some of the white plastic letters on the old sign, changing it from First Lutheran Church of Binder to plain old Church of Binder. It's not that her daddy had anything against the Lutherans, he just never chose one denomination over another.

Ollie thought his choice for the new name lacked originality, but Reverend Love was clear on the fact he wasn't soliciting opinions.

"Load them up, girls," Susanna said, teetering one shoofly pie in each hand. "And no stacking." The entire Chevy truck bed was being filled with the homemade delights, leaving no room for anyone to ride. The girls would walk alongside the truck as their mama and daddy slowly rolled it down the road, careful not to have the tires kick up dust on Mrs. Mahoney's flaky piecrust. She had told Ollie the secret was in the ice water and cold butter cubes she added to the mix. "You have to get the ingredients as cold as possible," she had said.

Yet another reason why a person shouldn't be required to live without refrigeration.

"This is a big day for you, Ollie," Camille said as they walked to the church.

"It's a big day for all of us."

"But especially for you. That's what Daddy said. He said it was big as in *of great importance*. Not big as in *large in bulk or number*."

Ollie looked down to her younger sister and wondered what their daddy had meant. Why it would be any more special for her than the other girls? They wanted this, too, didn't they? Well, all but Martha, who Ollie sincerely believed would come around in time. Once school began in the fall and she saw the benefits of staying put in a town. Once she made a few friends.

Reverend Love rounded the corner onto Main Street, where Ollie could see the Carter boys sitting at the card table next to their mama's store, playing another game of slapjack. They were in grubby jeans and undershirts, squashing Ollie's secret hope they'd change their ways and decide to join them for services.

Susanna lifted a delicate hand in hello as they rolled past the market where the boys sat. Ralph gave a short nod of his head, but Joseph snaked his lips into a smile.

Something about that smile didn't sit right with Ollie.

"Do you think they'll be more friend-like, now that we're staying?" Camille asked.

"Sure they will," Ollie said.

"Sure as right, sure as rain," Ellen said from behind them.

"Please don't tell me you honestly believe that," Martha said. "Those boys ain't never gonna like you, Camille. Or any of us, for that matter. Some people are just born mean."

"That's not true," Ollie and Gwen said at the exact same time. Then they passed each other a smile.

Just then, the Chevy came to a stop in front of the church where Jimmy was pacing back and forth in front of the main door. The way he walked and wrung his hands around each other reminded Ollie of Virginia in her cell.

Ollie jumped out of line and sprinted over to him. "What's wrong?"

"Gone, they're all gone." He was hardly breathing and pushed out the words in broken chunks.

"What's gone?"

By now, the other girls were around him, and

Reverend and Susanna Love were coming up the walk.

"My frogs," he said, panic and worry twisted up on his face. "When I got up this morning, all of their cartons were tipped over."

"Maybe they jumped real hard and knocked them down," Ellen said in her hopeful way. "Maybe they're at the marsh, waiting for you."

"Some of the cartons were torn," Jimmy said.

"We don't have time for this now," Martha said, hand on her hip. "This here is a big day for Ollie."

Since when did Martha care about Ollie's big day?

"Let's go inside," Reverend Love said. "We've got twenty minutes before the service to talk it through." He stepped past his girls and pulled the key from his pocket. Then he turned to Ollie. "I was going to have you do the honors," he said.

Ollie shot a look at Jimmy.

"Go ahead," he said.

Ollie took the key from her daddy's hand and went to slide it into the old lock. But as she pressed against the door, it swung open a tiny bit. The door was already unlocked. Ollie flashed a look of uncertainty at her daddy and then pushed the door wide.

No one moved.

That is, until Jimmy fell to his knees.

"Sweet Jesus, help us all," Susanna gasped.

Ollie turned and looked into the church.

Dead frogs lined every surface. They were cut open, pink entrails strewn along the pew backs. Ruby red blood smeared across the walls. Little green, gray, and brown bodies lying limp in the aisle and dangling over the podium.

Reverend Love stepped through the door. Ollie noticed his right fist clenching and opening, clenching and opening. The blue vein that ran down the side of his neck was pulsing with each movement.

Then she looked to Jimmy. He was stone silent, knees bent to the cement, head hanging heavy in his hands. What was going through his mind, she could not begin to imagine.

Susanna started herding the younger girls back toward the Chevy. "Come on," she said. "Step away. You don't need to see this side of people."

That's when Ollie realized it was real people who had done this. *Actual people.*

And she didn't have to think long to know who it was.

24

There wasn't time to clean up the bloodied frogs before the nine o'clock service. Reverend Love didn't even try; Jimmy's needs were more pressing. He wrapped his arm around the boy and led him over to the shade of that tupelo tree in the front churchyard. Ollie hung back and let them be alone. She looked on and noticed Jimmy's narrow shoulders, sagging and weighed down by sorrow, next to her daddy's thick, straight shoulders. The thought occurred to her that God made her daddy's shoulders broad and strong so he could hold up the burdens of others.

When people arrived, Reverend Love gave a brief explanation as to why services would be canceled and then returned to Jimmy's side.

But he did not close the church door.

It was left open for anyone who wanted to

wander over and see. It was left open as a testament to all that had gone wrong in the town.

Susanna gave soft pats to shoulders and tried to offer comfort as people walked to the door, looked inside, and then stepped away. Mrs. Mahoney clicked her tongue and told her neighbors that change was long overdue.

Ollie sat on the Chevy's tailgate, away from everyone else. She swung her legs and looked up to heaven. She bit her lip and held back the tears that wanted to spill out all over her face. She controlled her anger and told herself it would do no good to cause a scene.

Gwen wandered over to where she was sitting and leaned up against the side of the truck bed. "You all right?" she asked.

Ollie nodded.

Gwen was twisting a piece of grass in her hands. "Jimmy'll be okay. Daddy's with him. He has that special way with people when they're low." She looked up. "It's a gift how he can lift people's spirits."

Ollie couldn't help but think that Gwen had the same gift, coming over with her soothing words.

"I'm not saying it's easy," Gwen went on, "but he'll work through it. You'll see."

Camille came over to the truck and joined her sisters. She climbed up on the tailgate next to Ollie and leaned her head on Ollie's shoulder without a single word. Gwen stepped over and jumped up onto the tailgate as well.

Martha came next, Ellen at her side. "Scoot over," she said, all curt, acting like she was doing them a big favor. Ollie could see right through her fake huff and scooted over to let her sit. Ellen stood at Ollie's swinging feet until Ollie reached her hands out and pulled her baby sister onto her lap.

There they sat, all five sisters, crammed on the Chevy tailgate, swinging legs and staring off across the field and saying nothing, but feeling everything. Then Martha reached into her dress pocket and pulled out her harmonica. She held it to her lips, drew in a slow breath, and began playing "Rock of Ages."

Gwen sang, just above a whisper, "Rock of Ages, cleft for me, let me hide myself in thee."

And while she sang, Ollie let her tears fall.

• • •

When most everyone had left, Ollie slid off the tailgate and turned back toward the church.

Both Sheriff and Ray Burton were standing on the step. She was surprised to see them wearing clean, buttoned-up shirts—as if they had come dressed for services. More so, she was surprised to see each of them carrying a bucket of soapy water.

"You take your family home, Reverend," Sheriff Burton said. "My boy and I will take care of this."

Reverend Love stood up. "We don't mind doing our part."

"This here's town business."

"And we are part of this town now, sheriff."

Sheriff Burton lifted his chin and looked long at Reverend Love. "So you are," he said. "If you'd like, we'd be happy to clean this up so the boy there doesn't have to. But if you choose to stay, we'd be obliged for the help."

Reverend Love walked over to the sheriff. "It is I who am obliged," he said, placing a strong and grateful hand on the sheriff's shoulder.

They turned and went into the church. Jimmy began to follow. Ollie reached out and stopped him. "No," she said.

Jimmy shrugged her off. "I got to." He walked up the steps, steadied himself for a moment at the door, and then went in.

Susanna thought Ellen and Camille were too young to help with the cleanup, so she drove them and the pies and salads back to Mrs. Mahoney's. Jimmy, the rest of the Love family, Mrs. Mahoney, and the Burtons worked together cleaning the church and setting each lifeless frog body along the exterior wall in a tidy row, side by side, stretching the length of the building.

Ray Burton dug a trench in front of the frogs—deep enough for a proper burial—and Jimmy tenderly placed each frog in the earth, tumbling the hot summer soil back over them as he went. Martha came behind him and dressed each frog's grave with a single wildflower. Gwen had set to collecting the flowers in the adjacent field.

It took the rest of the day, but eventually the church looked fresh again. If it weren't for the row of tilled soil and strewn flowers that stretched in a straight line along the east wall, there would be no evidence of what had occurred.

Sheriff Burton wiped his brow with the back of his arm. "Now, if you'll excuse me," he said, "I have some business to take care of."

Ollie begged Jimmy to stay the night at Mrs. Mahoney's with her family, but he wanted to be back up the holler. He even refused to let her walk him home. She could imagine him sitting in the middle of his frog ranch, tattered and empty milk cartons all around. She wanted to be there with him, to give him the strength he'd need.

But he wanted to be alone.

And sometimes there's nothing more a person can do. So Ollie watched her friend walk on past Mrs. Mahoney's house, turn up the road to Mason's Holler, and disappear from view.

• • •

The next couple of days passed slowly and painfully for Ollie. Jimmy stayed away, and her mama and daddy refused to let her go find him, saying he needed time and would come back when he was ready.

There was still much work to be done at Mrs. Mahoney's, so Ollie and her sisters pruned flower bushes and fertilized the soil. It soothed them to "lose themselves in the service of others," as their daddy had so often preached. And it kept their minds from being idle and wondering what was happening with Jimmy or Virginia or what Sheriff Burton was doing to punish those Carter boys.

But the thing that was hardest for Ollie was seeing her daddy sulk around the house. He tried to hide it, to show a happy face, but Ollie knew better. She noticed how he was humming and singing less. How he spent more time standing in Mrs. Mahoney's field that was behind her house, staring off toward the highway.

The Thursday after Jimmy disappeared up the holler, Ollie was sitting on the porch, watching her daddy stand out in the field gazing off down the road, when Martha sat down beside her.

"He ain't happy, you know," Martha said.

Ollie sat quiet.

"You can't take someone who was born for the road and tie them to a church. If you'd quit making googly eyes at Jimmy long enough to pay attention to anyone else in this family, you'd see that."

Ollie pressed her lips together and thought before she said, "He'll adjust."

"Maybe," Martha said. "But, *adjusting* and *living* aren't the same thing. I know we don't agree most of the time, and I don't expect you'll understand this, but I want you to know I miss how he used to be."

"Even if I did forget about Jimmy, Martha, what about Virginia? We can't let her rot in jail for a crime she didn't commit."

"Yeah, I know. Like I said, I didn't expect you to understand." Martha stood up, looked off at their daddy in the field, and then walked away.

Ollie stayed on that porch another hour, watching her daddy fixed out in the field. She couldn't imagine what he was doing. Or thinking. But then he took off toward town.

Ollie skipped up behind him, though not close enough to be noticed, and followed as her daddy walked down the road, turned onto Main Street, and took himself right up to Sheriff Burton's office.

"It's been four days, and you've not done a thing," Reverend Love said to the sheriff.

Ollie hung outside the door, listening.

"Well," Sheriff Burton said, his voice meandering down a slow line, "that's not true, preacher. It's not right what happened, and I've done my best to set it straight."

Reverend Love raised his voice a bit, something Ollie wasn't used to. "What have you done? There's been no arrest."

"On what grounds would I make an arrest?"

Ollie peeked in and saw the sheriff, leaning back in his chair, swirling that stump of a cigar that grew in the corner of his mouth. His son, Ray, sat in a chair by the bookshelf on the right.

"On the grounds they trespassed onto Jimmy Koppel's land and took his property and desecrated the church."

"I don't think a few bog frogs count as actual property," Sheriff Burton said. "And no permanent damage has been done to the church. It's been cleaned."

"So you are going to let them get away with it." It was a statement more than a question.

"Who's *them*, Reverend?"

"Those Carter boys!"

"Is that who you think did this?"

"Who else?" Reverend Love said. Ollie had never heard her daddy so contentious.

"Hmph." Sheriff Burton leaned forward on his desk and pulled his cigar from his mouth. "And here I had you nailed for a good judge of character."

"Was it not those boys?"

"'Those boys,' as you call them, have clean hands in this. The older one, Ralph, got accepted to the architecture program up at the university. He'll be heading out next week." Sheriff Burton was smiling and enjoying pointing out Reverend Love's mistake. "Seems you're wrong about all sorts of things. What else you reckon you been wrong about, preacher man?" He shoved the cigar back into his mouth and laughed.

Reverend Love turned to leave and stumbled over Ollie at the doorway. He didn't look surprised, or upset, to see her there.

"I think you folks have a right to know something," Sheriff Burton called out from his chair. "The bus'll be here for Virginia in five days. She's going to the penitentiary."

Ray Burton shot out of his chair. "Is that so, Daddy?"

Ollie was surprised to see such a reaction.

"I found the transfer papers buried down at the bottom of the filing drawer. Thought you had sent those out weeks ago." He was talking to Ray.

"I did," Ray said, skittery as all get out. "Or, um, I thought I did."

"Well, it don't matter," Sheriff Burton said. "I've corrected our mistake and just got word of the transfer date. Tuesday the sixth, at three p.m. It'll do the town good to have her out of here. Folks need to move on with their lives."

Reverend Love stood firm in the doorway of that office. "You know as well as I that woman is innocent."

"Might be," Sheriff Burton said. "But if she is, she's protecting the one person who isn't."

"Jimmy's innocent, too!" Ollie hollered.

"You go on believin' that."

"Does Jimmy know?" Ray asked his daddy.

"He does," Sheriff Burton said. "I told him when he came for his morning visit."

"I guess there's no changing things," Ray said.

Why does Ray care? Ollie wondered.

"Nope," his daddy answered.

Reverend Love and Ollie walked down the steps and on into town. When they had gone a ways, Ray stepped out from behind a rock wall.

"I gotta tell you something," he whispered, glancing over his shoulder.

"Does your daddy know you're here?" Reverend Love asked.

Ray shook his head. "I told him I was going home to pick up our lunch. I thought you should know it wasn't the Carter boys who took them frogs," he said. "It was their ma."

"Esther?" Reverend Love asked. "How do you know?"

"She wasn't ashamed to say what she'd done. Said you all deserved it for causing trouble. Said Jimmy deserved it just for being a Koppel." He was fidgeting and scuffing his boots in the grass, hands plunged deep into his jeans pockets. "It's not right, what she did. I just wanted to say that."

"But she's a grownup," Ollie said. "And Jimmy's just a kid."

"Don't matter to her," Ray said, darting a look over his shoulder once more. "I gotta go."

Reverend Love took Ray by the arm. "Thank you, son. We appreciate the information."

Ray disappeared around the back of the building.

Reverend Love led Ollie over to the rail fence and kudzu patch that held the summer lambs. The one Jimmy liked to sit in from time to time. "You all right?" he asked.

She was shaking her head. "I don't understand it, Daddy. I can see a fool boy doing something terrible like that. But an adult should know better."

"It's true, there's no excuse for what happened." Reverend Love pulled a tiny purple flower from the twisting vine that lined the road and offered it to his daughter. "But some people are broken. They don't know anything other than hatred." He paused and looked up at the searing blue sky. "It's like their heart gets going in the wrong direction early on in life, and they can never quite manage to bring it back around to love. It's a sad thing and we should have compassion for them. Think of the joy they are missing in life."

Ollie couldn't imagine having any compassion for Esther Carter. Not after what Ray had just told them. Even so, she stood up and nodded her head. "I'll try," she said.

Ollie and her daddy walked quietly back to Mrs.

Mahoney's. When they got there, Jimmy was at the gate. It was the first time they had seen him since the Sunday before.

"The bus is comin'," he said. His eyes were empty and sad. "Tuesday."

"There has to be something we can do," Ollie said, turning to her daddy. "We can't give up on her."

"It's over," Reverend Love said. "I've written the state officials and tried to bring reason to Sheriff Burton. Every effort leads us back where we began. As long as Virginia stands by her confession, our hands are tied." The creases around his gemlike eyes softened. "I'm truly sorry, Jimmy. I'm sure your aunt in Tennessee will offer you a good home and allow you to keep in touch with your mama as much as possible."

Frustration pulsed through Ollie's veins as she saw her daddy accept defeat.

She grabbed Jimmy by the arm and pulled him over to the side of the house. When she had taken him out a good distance from her daddy, she said, "I've got a notion Ray Burton knows something about what happened."

"What would Ray know?"

"I'm not sure, but he's involved somehow. I'm certain of it."

Jimmy kicked at the dusty road. "Your daddy's right, Ollie. It's over. Let it go."

Tiny thumps of anger started down at Ollie's toes, shot up her legs, through her torso, and right out her mouth. "And let your mama be shipped away? And watch you be carted off to live with an aunt who you don't even know? That's plain stupid!"

"There's nothing to be done." Jimmy's voice was raised to meet Ollie's.

"There is, too! Ray was the one who left those milk cartons and food on your doorstep. Mrs. Mahoney told me so. He was always slinking up that holler. He might have been there on the day your daddy was killed. He might have seen someone or something."

"Like what?"

"How would I know? But he's been slipping food to your mama ever since she's been in that jail, and it looked to me like he hid your mama's relocation papers at the bottom of his daddy's desk. Why, Jimmy? Why would he go out of his way to protect her? You should have seen him when he learned about the transfer—jumpy and full of questions. And he told me some other things, too."

"Like what?" Jimmy asked.

Ollie started to tell him about how Ray had said it was Esther Carter who slaughtered his frogs, but decided not to bring the incident up. She had just gotten Jimmy back. She didn't want to lose him to sorrow again. "I just have a feeling he knows something."

"He'd never tell us anything. It's Ray Burton, for cripe's sake!"

"I know, but I'm gonna figure this out. We've got five days."

Jimmy nodded. "Five days."

25

The following Sunday was beautiful. The sky was bathed in soft turquoise. The roses in Mrs. Mahoney's yard were every shade of pink you could possibly imagine, and bees hummed lazily through the patches of clover on the grass.

Ollie was worried folks would hold back and not come to services, given the horrible scene they had been met with the week before. They had lost so much lately, she wanted to give her daddy a full chapel. So she knelt by her shared bedside and said a simple prayer that the people of Binder would gather around them.

Jimmy walked to the church with the family. Reverend Love had gone an hour before, saying he needed time to prepare his sermon. Ollie thought he was going ahead to make sure everything was all right—to avoid any possible repeat of the prior week.

"You come up with any ideas?" Jimmy whispered to Ollie on their way to the church.

"Almost," Ollie said.

"What's 'almost' mean?"

"I'm working on something. I just need more time."

"We ain't got time. Two days, Ollie. Then my mama's gone. Two days."

Ollie nodded. "I know."

Ellen skipped up and took Jimmy's hand. "Whatcha whispering about?" she asked.

"Nothing," Ollie said.

"That's what Martha said! She said Jimmy's whispering sweet nothings to you."

Ollie felt her face flush red, but Jimmy just laughed. "Come closer, Ellen," he said. The girl stood on her tiptoes while Jimmy whispered in her ear, "Nothing, nothing, nothing, nothing."

Ellen giggled. "That tickles."

When they came upon the church, the group stopped for a moment. "Come on," Jimmy said. "It's all right." He led the way up the walk and through the front door.

It was quite a sight.

Sun was streaming through windows on both sides, laying down shafts of light against the dark wood floor. The pews were freshly oiled and shone so bright they'd pass for new. Mrs. Mahoney had clipped two vases of hydrangeas and roses and had them resting on either side of the podium, which stood tall and firm at the front. And behind it stood Reverend Love. Ollie thought her daddy looked perfect there, like God Himself was standing at that pulpit.

Susanna led them to the front row. They had barely sat down when Ollie heard people coming in behind her. At first, it was just adults coming in, but then Ollie saw something else. Something different.

The children of Binder started into the church. Each one carried a sawed-off milk carton, and each carton contained a single frog. They walked up to the front pew and sat the frogs down at Jimmy's feet. One by one, first ten, then twenty, then thirty-some frogs all clustered around him.

Jimmy looked at Ollie for answers, but she didn't know what was happening. They both looked up at her daddy, but he had a surprised look on his face as well. It was clear he was as clueless as they were.

Only Martha seemed to know what was going on. She directed the younger children on where to set their frogs and gave them a knowing nod as they stepped away.

Martha.

When the last frog had been placed at Jimmy's feet and the opening hymn was being sung, Ollie leaned over to her sister. "Why?" she asked.

Martha looked surprised by the question. "He lost everything," she whispered under the tones of song rising up to the church rafters. "His daddy, his mama, his frogs. Why wouldn't I help him?"

Ollie placed a hand on Martha's. "Thank you," she said. "It was very thoughtful."

"So blessed we are," Reverend Love began once the song had ended. "To be surrounded by loving neighbors."

"Neighbors," Camille whispered. "One's fellow man."

• • •

After the service, Reverend Love walked back to Mrs. Mahoney's, drove the Chevy over, loaded up the frogs, and took them up the holler with Jimmy and Ollie riding in the cab. They piled the old cartons up and burned them, along with some other trash. They set the new cartons in perfect rows. There weren't as many as Jimmy originally had, but he would enjoy their company, even if it was just for a few days.

"I sure enjoyed your sermon today, Reverend," Jimmy said.

"Thank you, son."

"Is it nice having a real congregation?"

Reverend Love didn't answer. He kept fidgeting with the last row of milk cartons, trying to get the line just so. Ollie knew he heard the question.

"'Cuz I was thinkin'," Jimmy continued, "that it must be nice for you to have a real congregation after all this time."

Reverend Love straightened his back and smiled. "I've always had a real congregation."

"I mean, one that doesn't change. And so many people there today! You'll be able to get your own place in no time."

Ollie knew Jimmy was happy and trying to share his joy, but could see her daddy wasn't taking it. It made her sad, and she thought again of what Martha had said, about how you can't change a person's wandering spirit. Maybe asking her daddy to stay was like asking a stream to sit and visit for a while. Nature just wouldn't allow it.

"Want to come for Sunday dinner?" Ollie asked Jimmy. "Mrs. Mahoney has made one of her pies, and Mama put some chicken soup on to simmer this morning."

"Nah," Jimmy said. "I've gotta give these guys something to eat."

"And tie a string on their foot so you recognize them the next time you meet?" Ollie asked.

Jimmy dropped his head. "No reason for that. I'll be leaving soon enough."

"I don't think you're going anywhere. I have an idea for dealing with that one situation." Ollie was trying to be vague so her daddy wouldn't know their suspicions of Ray Burton.

"Go on," Jimmy said.

Ollie looked over to her daddy, who was climbing into the truck. Then she whispered, "Meet me before first light at the cemetery—over by the bramble bushes along the south wall."

"For what?"

"Just be there."

· · ·

Ollie sat on Mrs. Mahoney's porch with a pencil in one hand and a pad of paper in the other. She kept flicking her pencil against the notepad, trying mightily to work out the details of her plan. Everything that made her Olivene Love was telling her Ray Burton had a hand in Henry Koppel's murder. He knew something, saw something. Somehow, he was involved.

What else she knew about Ray Burton was this—he was superstitious.

She knew it because of the way he skittered and danced when he saw that black cat on the day her daddy visited with Virginia. Ollie intended to use that information to her advantage.

She put lead to paper and wrote:

Though dead, I sleep not,
and soon you'll be caught.
Your secret I'll not save.

Your haunt will be mine
'til end of all time.
I'll make you sorrow's slave.

'Tis true you can bring
a stop to this thing.
Come at the dawn's first light.

And on my stone place
a token of grace:
a rose of purest white.

• • •

Ollie did not sleep that night. She tucked her shoes and clothes under the bed and lay with her eyes open until the clock showed four o'clock. She could not force her body to be still another minute.

Ever so slowly, ever so carefully, she inched out of bed, slipped on her clothes, and tiptoed down the staircase and out the front door. Cool night air danced around her body—energizing, calling, teasing. It was playful, but Ollie was not in the mood. *Please, Lord, allow the end to justify these means.* She had secretly delivered the note to Ray after supper. It would be his own fault if he showed. He would be telling on himself.

Ollie turned right at Mrs. Mahoney's gate and sprinted out past the row of limestone houses, past the entrance to Mason's Holler, and right up to the graveyard at the edge of town. A butterscotch moon hung in the blue-black sky and cast a yellow, sickly glow down on the rows of tombstones. Ollie forced herself to take a slow, deep breath and steady her jittery nerves. She reminded herself that a cemetery was a sacred place and that the dead were busy up in heaven singing hallelujahs and dancing with angels. They did not care about a girl sneaking around their stones in Binder, Arkansas. She was not superstitious.

"Hey," a voice cut in from behind her.

Ollie all but wet her drawers. "Shh!" she said to Jimmy, with a finger over her mouth.

"What's the big plan?" he whispered.

Ollie told Jimmy about the note she'd sent Ray

and how, as she figured it, he wouldn't come if he wasn't afraid of Henry's ghost and would come if he was.

"What if he's afraid of the ghost, but still doesn't know anything?" Jimmy asked.

"He knows."

The two scrambled over to the brick half-wall that lined the south side of the cemetery. They scrunched down behind the bramble bushes, pulling their knees in tight in an effort to make themselves small.

They sat that way for a long while.

"What if he doesn't come?" Jimmy asked.

"He'll come."

"But what if he doesn't?"

Ollie didn't answer, because Jimmy's question was followed by a soft crunch and shuffle of leaves. She lifted a finger to her lips once more.

"I know," Jimmy mouthed.

There in the indigo turn of morning, Ray Burton walked across the cemetery with a white rose trembling in his clutch. He went directly to Henry Koppel's grave and laid the bloom across the stone. "I done like you said," Ray said to Henry's dead body. "Just like you said. Now you can rest quiet." Ray's voice quivered out across the early morning.

Ollie hadn't figured on what she'd do next. She

didn't have time to think that far ahead, but it didn't matter. Jimmy sprang from his spot among the brambles and tackled Ray to the ground. Ollie scrambled after and tried to pull him off Ray, but Jimmy was swinging punches like he was Sugar Ray Robinson.

"Get off!" Ollie hollered, wrapping both arms around Jimmy's middle and pulling with all her might.

Jimmy kept punching. His fist slammed into Ray's stomach.

"Off!" Ollie hollered once more, still pulling.

"He killed my daddy!" Jimmy was screaming. Then he was crying. Then he seemed to lose all his strength and fell down next to the crumpled heap that was Ray Burton. Jimmy buried his sobbing face in his hands. "He killed my daddy."

Ollie helped Ray sit up.

The three sat on Henry's grave, right on the very top of it, for a long while. Jimmy was getting his emotions together, Ray was still doubled over, and Ollie was trying to squeeze herself between the two boys in an effort to create a little distance.

"Ray did *not* kill your daddy," Ollie said once the electricity in the air settled down to a low buzz. Then she saw a flash in Ray's eyes that told her the truth. "You didn't kill Henry, did you, Ray?"

Sweat was pushing out all around Ray's brow. "I had to," he said. "On account of what he was doing to Virginia, beatin' on her even though she was knocked out cold—even though she couldn't raise a hand in defense." Water rimmed his eyes and, embarrassed, he quickly shoved aside the tears with the palm of his hand. "I had to make him stop."

"What were you doing up the holler?" Ollie asked.

Ray dabbed a handkerchief to his bloody lip. "I felt sorry for them. So I collected a few things, crept up the holler, and secretly dropped them off from time to time. But I can't help it if Virginia jumped to a confession." Ray's jaw flinched. He steeled his eyes and said, "If that woman wants to throw her life away, 'tain't my job to fix it." He stood up, steadied his wobbly legs, and began to walk away. When he got to the edge of the cemetery, he turned back toward Ollie and Jimmy. "You don't got no evidence against me. Not one stitch."

26

Ray was right, of course. No one would believe Ollie and Jimmy's word against his, and Sheriff Burton had no reason to throw out Virginia's confession. They finally knew who killed Jimmy's daddy, but it didn't make any difference. Not only that, Ollie couldn't bring herself to fault Ray. Anyone in that situation would have done the same thing. The fact that his helping ended with the death of Henry Koppel was just a bad ending to a bad situation.

Jimmy told Ollie he felt like being alone and wandered back up Mason's Holler. Ollie slowly walked back to Mrs. Mahoney's.

She found her mama and daddy sitting on the front porch swing, holding hands and smiling into the fresh lemon light of morning.

"You're up and out early," her daddy said.

Ollie wasn't sure what to say. She needed to tell

him, of course, but didn't know where to begin. The words started out all right in her head but then melted into nothing on her tongue. Reverend Love knew his daughter well enough to see the seriousness of the situation. He nudged over to his wife and gave a firm pat to the empty spot on the swing. "Come sit."

Ollie sat.

Reverend Love reached his arm around Ollie and gave another push to the white wooden swing. Its chains creaked under the weight of the three Loves. A black bumblebee bobbled lazily around the swing chain.

"Nice day," Reverend Love said.

"Nearly perfect," Ollie's mama agreed.

"Terrible news about Virginia Koppel, though," Reverend Love continued. "She'll be leaving tomorrow. I guess we couldn't be much help after all."

"Well," Ollie's mama said. "We were able to offer some relief. Sometimes that's all a person can do."

"I know who did it," Ollie said. She meant the words to come out strong and believable. Instead, they scratched out of her dry throat and quickly floated to the ground.

"All right then," her daddy said.

"It was Ray Burton."

"The sheriff's son?" Reverend Love asked.

"You see the problem."

Ollie told her parents how she'd tricked Ray out to the cemetery based on his superstitions.

"That wasn't nice," her daddy said.

"I know," Ollie answered. "But I couldn't think of anything else. If Ray didn't show, then I would have known he was innocent. If he did show, well . . . then he'd be telling on himself."

"There's truth to that," Susanna said with a nod. "I think it was downright clever."

Then Ollie told them what Ray said—how he came upon Henry Koppel beating his knocked-out wife and how he had to make it all stop. She told them about the milk cartons, food, and fabric that Ray took up to the Koppel place. She reminded them how Ray "accidentally" forgot to mail off the prison transfer papers, and how Ollie thought it was all because he didn't want Virginia going to the state penitentiary for a crime she didn't commit.

All the while Ollie talked, her parents listened. When she came to the end, Reverend Love rubbed his stubbly chin and nodded his head. "It seems to me Ray is the only person who can help Virginia."

"He won't," Ollie said. "He said it wasn't his fault she jumped in and signed a confession. He said it wasn't his job to stop her if she wanted to throw her life away." Ollie shook her head. "I still don't get why she signed that confession."

"They were bound to take one of them," Reverend Love said. "She knew this town well enough to know Sheriff Burton would make his arrest without seeking out the truth. Both Jimmy and his mama certainly had motive. I suppose she protected her son the only way she knew how."

"Well, now she's stuck. Ray is never going to tell on himself, and his daddy is never going to believe a word we say."

"Well," Reverend Love said, leaning back in the swing, "I wouldn't say never. It's plain the boy has goodness in him. I guess it's our job to help him find courage as well. We'll think of something."

• • •

Mrs. Mahoney had books piled high in all the corners of her library. Dust and books, books and dust. Ollie ran her finger along the spines of those books and imagined the lives that hid within those pages. Lives with happy endings—all neatly tied up in a bow. Lives with answers to questions and justice for all. If only real life could be like that. Ollie was learning it wasn't even close.

Ellen came skipping in with Baby Doll Sue tucked under one armpit and Mrs. Mahoney's Madelyn tucked under the other. She was singing "Mama's Little Baby" at the top of her voice.

"*Please*, Ellen," Ollie said from her place at the bookshelf.

"Please porridge hot, please porridge cold, please porridge in the pot nine days old."

Ollie rolled her eyes and turned back to the books. She was hoping to find one that might give her an idea—any idea. Her well had run completely dry.

"Excuse me," Ellen said with a sassy shake of her hip.

"Sorry," Ollie said. "I'm trying to think."

"'Bout how to save Jimmy's mama?"

"Yes, about how to save Jimmy's mama."

"Martha says she's beyond savin'."

Ollie tugged at a book, skimmed it, and returned it to its spot on the shelf. "Martha would say that, wouldn't she?"

"She says the bus'll come tomorrow."

"That's true," Ollie said.

"Why is Mrs. Carter so bad?" Ellen asked.

"She's not bad," Ollie said. "She's just scared."

Ellen tilted her head and gave her big sister a quizzical look.

"It's true. The town is mad at her for being so

mean. Things are changing here in Binder. Folks are tired of letting one or two people make everyone look bad."

"And feel bad," Ellen said.

"Yes," Ollie said. "And feel bad, too. Does that make any sense, Ellen?"

"Yeah," Ellen said. She skipped off down the hallway, leaving Ollie alone in Mrs. Mahoney's library. Ollie stared off across the room and watched dust flit and float in the sunlight streaming through the eyelet curtains.

Then the thought came to her. She would have to go see Virginia.

• • •

Ray lit out of his rocking chair when Ollie landed her feet on the steps of the sheriff's office.

"What do you want?" he asked, fear flickering in his eyes.

"I've come to see Virginia."

Ray put himself between the front door and Ollie. "Why don't you go on home? Better yet, why don't you pack up your family and leave altogether?"

Ollie remembered the tears in Ray's eyes when he confessed. She wasn't afraid of him. He was like one of Jimmy's frogs, puffing his chest and croaking loud. She shifted to the right, and then when Ray stepped over to block her, she ducked under his arm and slipped into his daddy's office.

"Afternoon, Sheriff Burton," she said, bright as cherry pie.

Sheriff Burton grumbled and kept his face down to the stack of papers on his desk. Ollie went down the stairs that led to the basement cells. Virginia Koppel was curled up in a ball on a feed sack, sleeping.

Ollie looked at the woman, nestled on a burlap sack in the middle of a patch of hay, and remembered a fat wren who had once fixed her nest to the bumper of their travel trailer. She laid three brownish pink eggs in her nest and watched over them faithfully. However, once the featherless babies hatched, the mama bird disappeared. Maybe it was the crowds that kept coming to the field, or maybe it was the smoke from the campfire, no one knew. Whatever the reason, she was gone, and her baby birds were left alone in the nest. Gwen tried to feed them ground-up worms and bits of seeds, but it was no use. They shriveled and died by the end of the first week. Ollie thought how Jimmy's mama looked something like those abandoned birds. All alone in her nest.

Ollie sat down on her side of the cell bars and cleared her throat. Virginia nearly jumped out of her skin at the tiny noise. She instinctively raised her hand to shield her face and called out, "Sorry." She wasn't even fully awake yet. It broke Ollie's heart to think anyone would have to start out each waking moment with an apology for just being. That was the legacy Henry Koppel left his wife.

"It's me, Mrs. Koppel. Ollie."

Virginia sat up and rubbed her sleepy eyes. "Is it time to go?"

"Not yet."

"You got some more of dem biscuits?"

"Not this time."

"Zucchini chips?"

"No," Ollie said. "We need to talk about your confession."

Ollie whispered the truth of what happened to Virginia between two black iron bars. She told how Ray had come upon Henry, and how Ray was trying to make him stop. She told her how she thought Ray might have confessed if Virginia hadn't signed the confession so quickly.

"Better you bring biscuits next time," Virginia Koppel said once Ollie had finished her story.

"But don't you see?" Ollie said, bursting with frustration. "If you deny your confession, and if we tell what we know, Ray will have to take his punishment."

"You're the one who don't see," Virginia said. "You think that sheriff up there's gonna put his own boy in jail? It don't matter what you know—or think you know."

"It's the truth!"

Virginia laughed. "I told you, no one cares 'bout no truth 'round here. Least of all Tommy Burton."

"But I care," Ollie said. "Jimmy cares. He needs you."

"What my boy needs is his freedom."

"You aren't giving him anything by allowing yourself to sit in jail for a crime you weren't even conscious for!" Ollie's voice was lifting, and she heard Sheriff Burton shuffle his feet by the door.

"No antagonizing the prisoners," he called down.

Ollie lowered her voice. "You are the only one who can turn this around. It's time for you to speak your truth."

"I'm a Koppel. That's my truth." She turned and lay back down on the feed sack, pulling her knees tight into her chest. "Now, if you'll excuse me," she said, "I hear it's a long ride to Little Rock, and I might need some rest."

27

Ollie met her mama on the road back to Mrs. Mahoney's. Susanna was wearing her purple dress and had her pearl hairpins tucked neatly around her curls. It wasn't an everyday outfit, and Ollie guessed her mama was up to something.

"She won't budge," Ollie said as she met her mama on the path, talking about Virginia.

"No," Susanna said. "I didn't think she would."

Ollie's lungs deflated. "But why?"

"Sometimes we have to meet people where they are, Ollie. Honor their desires, regardless of our own."

"Like when Daddy honored my desire to stay in Binder?"

Susanna stopped walking. "Your daddy and I wanted to give you this experience," she said. "It means so much to you."

"Not as much as seeing him happy means to me."
To her great surprise, she believed her own words.

"I'll let that be a discussion between you two."

"But, Mama, can I ask you a question?"

"Of course."

"Am I the only one who wanted to stay?"

Susanna didn't answer. Instead, she put her arm around Ollie's shoulder and said, "There's so much in this world we will never understand. But that doesn't mean that we give up trying. Come with me."

"Where are we going?"

"To do what we can."

Susanna guided her daughter back down Main Street, past the Seed and Feed, past the empty schoolhouse and the quilting cottage, all the way to the front door of Carter's Fresh.

"What are we doing here?" Ollie asked, certain her mama had lost her mind.

"The right thing," Susanna said. She tugged at her skirt, gave a gentle pat to her curls, and walked into Esther Carter's store. Ollie shadowed her mama.

Mrs. Carter was behind the counter, reading a newspaper. When she saw the Love women, she slowly folded the newspaper into a square and crossed her arms across her chest. "Well, well, well," she began. "What brings you here?"

Susanna said, "I'm here to settle the Koppels' account."

The only thing that matched the look of surprise on Esther Carter's face was the one hanging on Ollie's.

"If you will kindly show me their tab," Susanna continued, "I'd like to make things right."

"You ain't got that kind of cash," Esther Carter said. "They run up a bill of pert' near fifty dollars."

Susanna reached into her white pocketbook and pulled out a stack of faded green bills. Ollie's eyes bugged like a grasshopper. "I will pay their bill on one condition."

"Speak on," Esther Carter said, wary.

"I want you to promise me that you won't speak ill of the Koppel family any longer and that you'll show the boy some kindness for the brief time he has left in Binder."

"Why do you care so much if he's leaving?" Esther Carter asked.

"I want to clear the boy's name and give him a fresh start as he moves on."

"And if I refuse?"

"Then the bill goes unpaid. You know as well as I that Jimmy does not have the ability to ever pay this tab, especially with him leaving for Tennessee.

If you want your money, Mrs. Carter, you'll have to turn the other cheek."

Esther Carter rubbed her chin and pushed her tobacco from one cheek to the other with her tongue. She spit in her coffee can, lifted a small notebook, and said, "Let me see, they owe me forty-eight dollars and twenty-seven cents."

Susanna handed over the stack of bills. "There is fifty dollars there."

"So I owe you seventy-three cents in change."

"No," Susanna said. "You would owe me one dollar and seventy-three cents."

"Just checkin'," Mrs. Carter said. "But I guess you ain't dim-witted like that one girl of yours."

Ollie saw a spark of anger flicker in her mama's eyes. "Camille is not dim-witted. She is, on the contrary, quite gifted."

Mrs. Carter slid the money off the counter and put it into her till. "From what I can see, that girl's downright weird. Always carrying that dictionary around and spoutin' off definitions like anyone gives a plug nickel about what she has to say."

It was clear the woman was being hateful for the sport of it.

"But," Mrs. Carter continued, "if you say that's *gifted*, then I guess I won't disagree."

Susanna Love twisted in her spot. Little sideways swishes, like she was a soda bottle full of fizz and Mrs. Carter had just shaken her good. "You seem," she began, pacing her words, "so full of hatred. It's quite a pity."

"I ain't got no hatred, lady."

"You hate the Koppels," Susanna said.

"That's just common sense."

"You've shown hatred toward our family and Camille's gift."

"Well, that girl is plain crazy. Everyone can see that."

"You hate the church."

"Who doesn't hate church?"

"You are a bitter woman and, frankly, I feel sorry for you."

That did it. Mrs. Carter slammed her fist onto the counter and leaned over into Susanna's face.

Susanna didn't flinch.

"We was fine in this town 'til your family came along, spreading rumors and stirring up trouble."

"Rumors? What rumors did we ever spread?"

"It's all over how I hurt that boy's frogs. My business done dropped by half."

Ollie was happy to hear it.

"Rumor," Susanna said in her best Camille

impression. "A statement without discernible knowledge of the truth."

"What's that act supposed to mean?"

"It means if you have lost business due to a real action, and a despicable one at that, it is not based on any rumor. It is, rather, a natural consequence of your own making." With that, Susanna turned and left Carter's Fresh for the last time.

Ollie held her tongue until they were nearly back to Mrs. Mahoney's. "Where'd you get that money?" she asked.

"Mrs. Mahoney was kind enough to drive me over to an antique shop in Coleville this morning," her mama said very matter-of-factly. "I sold Nana Shirlene's platter."

"The one with the red roses?"

"Yes."

"The one that was your great-great-grandmother's?"

"You know the one," Susanna said.

"But, Mama, that was the best thing you had."

Susanna took her daughter by both hands and looked into her eyes. "No," she said. "You, your sisters, and your daddy are the best things I have. That, Ollie, was just a plate."

28

Later that evening, Ollie's parents allowed her to go up the holler, knowing Jimmy might need a friend on this last night before his mama was shipped off. He had spent the whole day with her at the jail, but now visiting hours were over and he had been sent home. She found him at Moody's.

"My daddy thinks we might be able to get Ray to 'fess up," she said, sitting down on the porch steps between Jimmy and Moody.

"Your daddy don't know much about the Burtons," Jimmy said.

"Ain't that the truth," Moody agreed. He was rubbing an oiled cloth across the grain of his trinket box, making the lines and swirls in the hickory wood come alive.

"My daddy said we have to help Ray find his

courage," Ollie said. "He says Ray can't be all bad, since he went around collecting those milk cartons and food out of the goodness of his own heart."

"And the scrap fabric," Jimmy said. "Mama would stitch it into pieces big enough to do something. She has one apron made up of a hundred scraps. It's my favorite. And the way he helped me bury my frogs. That was real nice."

Moody flipped the clasp of the box open and closed, inspecting its every detail. "There's truth in that, too," he said.

The three sat quietly on the steps and wondered how it was that you helped a person find courage. Ollie closed her eyes and remembered her mama paying off the Koppels' grocery tab to give Jimmy a fresh start. She thought how Mrs. Mahoney had offered up her land for him to farm. So much goodness going around . . . how could they get Ray Burton to see the light?

"So alone, forlorn and aching," Moody began mindlessly singing, lost in his handiwork.

"Reaching for the reverent light.
Reach on out, God's love will save you.
Save your soul, lead you aright."

"That's it!" Ollie jumped up and started running down the holler. "Meet me at sunrise," she called back to Jimmy. "In front of the Burtons' place. Don't be late."

"I'm never late."

• • •

The sheriff and Ray lived in a tall, skinny house that sat directly east of the sheriff's office. It was red brick, with white shutters. Ollie, her family, Mrs. Mahoney, and Jimmy gathered in the first light of morning on the dewy grass that spread out from the front door.

Reverend Love was holding Gwen's Bible and had it open to the Beatitudes. Gwen stood at his side, overflowing with joy and purpose.

"'Blessed are the peacemakers,'" Reverend Love called out, voice slicing through the stillness.

He closed his book and started singing. At first, the music was low and rumbled along the grass, but soon his voice lifted up and was joined by the voices of his family, calling out to all who had ears to hear.

And out they came. Lights flickered on in dim windows. Faces found their way through the split of curtains, and people stepped out onto their front porches. The Love family kept singing and, as they did, they noticed some of the townsfolk joining them in song. Tenors, altos, baritones, and basses mingled voices, praising the early cinnamon sun and adding to the sweet spirit of day. Ollie heard a buttery voice slide up behind her. She turned to see Moody standing in the pink light of dawn. He tilted his head and winked at her. Ollie's heart filled with joy at the sight of the old man. She stepped back and took his hand, all the while singing out strong. When the song ended, half of Binder was out in the street—including the Burtons.

"What is the meaning of this?" Sheriff Burton said, fixing the final loop on his trouser belt.

"We bring inspiration," Reverend Love said.

Ray Burton fidgeted on the step of his house.

Reverend Love began singing again, only this time it was a solo. He sang "Just As I Am," and the rich tones of his deep voice rang out a call for truth.

> "Just as I am, and waiting not
> to rid my soul of one dark blot . . ."

Reverend Love finished his song and turned to Ray. "Son," he said, "we shall wait no longer. Today is the day for you to lift your burden and share your truth."

Ray Burton wiped his sweaty palms against the sides of his blue jeans. He licked his skinny lips. He gave the tiniest shake of his head and looked down at Jimmy. The two boys met eyes and stared at each other for a long minute.

Ollie could see the invisible words being passed between them. Words of want and sorrow, pain and fear. Words of hope and prayer and courage.

Finally, Ray spoke up.

"I killed Henry Koppel," he said. "I didn't mean to, but I'm to blame."

Relief flooded through Ollie's veins and she smiled at Ray, who had found his courage after all.

"It's a lie!" Esther Carter called out from the crowded street.

"It's the truth," Ray said, empowered. "I was taking a load of milk cartons up to the Koppel place. I took them things I knew they needed from time to time." He licked his lips again and continued. "I came up to the house and heard Henry beatin' on Virginia. Only Virginia was knocked out cold on the ground." Ray began pleading with his father. "Honest, Pa, I thought he would kill her. I *knew* he would."

"What'd you do, son?" Reverend Love coaxed from his spot on the grass.

Ray answered, "I hollered for him to stop. Henry looked up and saw me in the window. His whole face was red with hatred. He charged toward the front door, so I ran out behind the woodpile. Henry saw me and ran after me. He was drunk, too. I could smell the whiskey on him. He lifted a log and chucked it at my head, but I ducked it off." Ray paused and looked at Jimmy again. "I asked him to stop, I begged him to, but he wouldn't. He ran at me and tripped over a stump. There was an ax wedged in a log, and Henry smacked his head right against the butt of it. I rolled him over, to help him, but I could see there was nothing to be done. The side of his head was split clean open." Ray paused one more time before finishing. "I dragged his body down to the river, trying to get him away from the house—hoping to make it look like an accident." Tears were streaming down his face. "How was I to know Virginia would sign a confession?" Ray lifted his wrists. "You can take me. I'm the one who needs to be going to Little Rock."

Sheriff Burton looked like his son had struck him across the face. "Is this true?"

"Yes," Ray said. "I am sorry, Pa. I didn't mean to cause so much trouble."

"No trouble in sharing truth," Reverend Love said in his clear voice. "You saved a woman's life. Isn't that right, sheriff?"

"I suppose that could be true."

"It is," Reverend Love said with surety. "Henry Koppel wasn't murdered. His own drunken meanness killed him. If he fell and cracked his head on an ax, it's not Ray's doing."

Ollie loved hearing her daddy speak with such fortitude.

"But I was there," Ray said. "And I caused him to charge at me, and then I moved his body down to the river . . . Isn't that being an accomplice or something?"

"Acts of courage," Reverend Love said. Murmurs of approval rose up from the street. "You were helping a neighbor, protecting a friend. You should be celebrated, Ray, not punished."

Ray dropped his head and sobbed.

His pa wrapped his arms around him. "It's over now," was all he said.

29

Sheriff Burton said he'd take care of the paperwork, allowing Jimmy and his mama to go home. Susanna followed with a kettle of chicken noodle soup and jars of plum jam. She spent the next few days up the holler, sweeping floors and mending curtains. Mrs. Mahoney reminded everyone Jimmy was free to farm her land, which gave new hope and promise to the situation.

Ollie took a break from helping her mama and found her daddy under the Chevy, changing the oil. "She doesn't get much use these days," she said, patting a tire on the old truck.

Reverend Love slid out from underneath the vehicle and sat up, wiping his oily hands on a dishrag. "No, I guess she doesn't."

"But it doesn't have to be that way, Daddy. Maybe

we should take her out on the road again. You know, set her free."

"Olivene Love, what are you talking about?"

Ollie thought for a moment. "I'm saying I think we should go back to the preaching road."

"No, child. We said we'd give it a year and then decide. That's the plan."

"But you're not happy here."

"Who said? I'm perfectly happy here."

Ollie knew when her daddy was lying. "Well," she said, "I'm not happy here." She held his gaze and tried to look as honest as possible.

"You're not?"

Ollie swallowed hard. "No, sir."

"Well, that's certainly something to think about."

"And I've talked to the others. They want to go as well."

"Do they?" Her daddy had a sparkle to his words again.

"Yes, but on one condition."

"My children are giving me conditions?"

"It's that Gwen gets to learn the trade."

Reverend Love leaned forward. "What do you mean?"

"Gwen. She wants to be a preacher, Daddy." Had he really not noticed? "Why do you think she studies the Scriptures so much? Why do you think she follows you around, copying your every move and digging your old sermons out of the trash after you've finished them?"

"Gwen does that?"

"Yes, Daddy!"

"Why hasn't she come to me?"

"She's afraid you'll say no, seeing how she's a girl and all."

Reverend Love leaned back and rubbed his chin. "Lord Almighty. A preacher girl." He looked over at Ollie. "I say we give it a try."

• • •

Reverend Love gassed up the Chevy truck and hitched the travel trailer.

Ollie followed her mama up Mason's Holler one last time to say goodbye to her friends. The family would say goodbye to Mrs. Mahoney when they were finished—when they could stand together and tell her how much her kindness meant. When they could circle around her and promise to keep in touch.

Jimmy was sitting on Moody's steps.

"I'll go on and see Virginia," Susanna said to her daughter. "You can stay here."

Ollie nodded and walked over to sit down next to Jimmy. She sat close and rested her head on his shoulder. The pungent smell of Rutger's Marsh lifted off his orange T-shirt. "I'll miss you," she said.

Jimmy brushed the hair from Ollie's face, gently running his fingers through her curls. "You know where I am. Someday, you'll come back."

Ollie couldn't bring the words. She nodded and tried to swallow the lump that was pushing into her throat.

"We'll be all right, Mama and me," Jimmy said out of the silence. "Mrs. Mahoney said I can grow watermelons in her field next year and sell them, and Mary Knuttal offered Mama a job at the quilting cottage. Now that my pa is gone, she's free to find her life again."

"Where's Moody?" Ollie asked.

"Inside."

Ollie knocked on the door. "I came to say good-bye," she said when it opened.

Moody reached out and took Ollie's hand, pressing his trinket box into her palm. "You listen to that preacher daddy of yours," he said. "He'll lead you right."

Ollie wrapped her fingers around the box.

"And don't forget the boy," Moody said. "Send a letter when you can."

"I will."

"You did good here, 'Olivene Love, oldest daughter of the Reverend Everlasting Love.' Real good."

Ollie smiled at the memory of their first meeting. "Thanks."

Moody turned back inside and Ollie sat down on the steps.

Jimmy took her hand and tied a line of cream-colored string around her wrist. "So I recognize you the next time we meet."

Ollie noticed a tiny wisp of a smile curling in the corner of his mouth.

"We're mighty grateful," Jimmy went on. "That music your daddy sang—it changed our lives."

"I know," Ollie said, voice feather soft. "Daddy says it's his trademark, but it's not. It is our only salvation."

Acknowledgments

In a book about family, it is a joy to thank those members of mine who have been extraordinarily patient during this writing adventure. I am grateful to my mother, Sarah Hart. I'll never forget the night, many years ago, when she happened upon me reading *Little Women* far past bedtime and gave me a book light instead of a lecture.

I have been blessed with the support of my husband, David, and three angel children, Meagan, Eli, and Claire. They have put up with "fix-your-owni" dinners night after hungry night.

A special thanks goes to Steven Chudney, my super agent, and to Margaret Ferguson, Susan Dobinick, and the insightful team at Farrar Straus Giroux. I was amazed to learn they love Ollie's story as much as I do. That is a wonderful feeling.

SQUARE FISH

WITH A NAME LIKE LOVE
by Tess Hilmo

Discussion Questions

1. Ollie's family travels from town to town without a house to call home. Discuss the pros and cons of this kind of lifestyle. Would this work for your family?

2. Early in the novel, Ollie says, "Everyone's got some goodness in them." Do you think this is true? Why or why not?

3. Ollie has four sisters: Martha, Gwen, Camille, and Ellen. How would you describe each one?

4. What do the townspeople think about Jimmy? Why does Ollie want to befriend him?

5. Discuss the role that Jimmy's frogs play in his life and in the story.

6. When you first meet Virginia Koppel, does she seem like she could have murdered her husband? Why do you think she would confess to doing so?

7. Who do you think set fire to the Loves' campsite?

8. Why does Mrs. Mahoney invite the Loves to stay with her? How do Ollie and her sisters feel about living in a house?

9. How does Ollie feel about the possibility of staying on in Binder? How does her daddy feel about it—and about having a church of his own?

10. Describe the incident when the Loves open the church doors for the first day of services. How did this make you feel? What do you think about the way Reverend Love handled it? Did Sheriff Burton and Ray's actions surprise you?

11. How does Ollie use Ray's superstitious nature to her advantage?

Questions by Leigh Courtney

GO FISH

TESS HILMO

© Jenni Howell Photography

What did you want to be when you grew up?
I wanted to be a star on Broadway! The problem is, I can't carry a tune, and—apparently—that matters to Broadway producers. Picky, picky.

When did you realize you wanted to be a writer?
I wrote a jailhouse love story in fifth grade because, at ten, I felt I was an expert on both prison life and love.

What's your favorite childhood memory?
I grew up with a mother who is an explorer at heart. We spent many nights camping on the beaches of California. I look back on those nights of campfire songs and tent giggles as some of my best memories.

What was your favorite thing about school?
I loved reading time in elementary school and then drama and speech in junior high and high school. Any excuse to pretend or use my imagination!

What were your hobbies as a kid?

I had a couple of goats as pets when I was younger. Waking up at five thirty a.m. to give them their breakfast was a challenge, but I loved playing with them and teaching them to follow me around town without using any kind of leash. That was pretty cool.

What was your first job?

My first job was at Baskin Robbins Ice Cream. My favorite combinations were coconut with hot fudge (tastes just like a Mounds bar!) and daiquiri ice with pineapple (a tangy bite of heaven!).

What book is on your nightstand now?

Liar and Spy by Rebecca Stead—it is brilliant so far!

How did you celebrate publishing your first book?

I had a carnival-themed party. There was a huge prize wheel, an old-fashioned candy counter, a friendship bracelet station, and a children's choir, which sang some of the gospel music from the book plus Moody's song (an original composition . . . you can hear the music for it on my Web site). What fun!

Where do you write your books?

Two places. If my children are at school, I write in my home office, but if it is summertime and they are home, I go to our local hospital. Don't laugh! It is a perfect place to write: comfy chairs, quiet lobbies, free Wi-Fi, vending machines, and clean restrooms—plus they are open all night.

What sparked your imagination for *With a Name Like Love*?

I like to write songs and have a deep respect for Southern gospel music. Years ago, I wrote my own song patterned after those old classic spirituals in pentatonic meter. When I played it for my mom on the piano, she said, "Tess, you should write a story to go with that song." And I did. *With a Name like Love* is that story, and my original song is actually Moody's song featured in the novel.

What about the setting appealed to you?

Who doesn't love a Southern setting? I have always been drawn to books and movies set in the South. It is rich with history and character, which makes my job as a writer easier. I specifically chose Arkansas because I have paternal ancestors from that area.

Have you ever lived in a town like Binder?

I grew up in Southern California and can recall moving nine times by my fourteenth birthday! Some towns were smaller than others, but none were as remote or confined as Binder. Still, I guess Ollie's longing for a home may have stemmed from my own similar longing as a child.

What was the most difficult and most rewarding parts of writing this novel?

The most difficult by far was overcoming the limitations we often put upon ourselves as writers or artists. Could I write a novel-length work? If I did, would it ever get published? If a publisher picked it up, would anyone bother to read it? I had to let the negative emotions go and focus on the story.

That was difficult at times. The best part continues to this day . . . it is hearing from actual readers. I am amazed when I open my mailbox and see a card or note from someone who enjoyed the book. I giggle and smile for days on end when that happens!

Which of your characters is most like you?

Often, people will ask me if Ollie is anything like me. I guess parts of her are from somewhere deep inside, especially her longing for a fixed-to-the-ground home. But I identify most with Jimmy. His life is not perfect. He has challenges and fears. Still, he believes in himself. One of my favorite scenes from the book is when Ollie asks Jimmy if he wants to leave Binder. Jimmy tells her a story of how he got lost in a thicket of hawthorn bushes right outside his back door. He said, "It may be a mess of thorns, but it's home." I just love that boy.

What makes you laugh out loud?

My children. They are total goofballs.

What do you do on a rainy day?

Weather in Utah is wild. We get amazing rain and lightning storms in the summertime. I like to pull my family out onto our back deck and watch the storms pass by. Sometimes it gets too intense and we have to go back inside. In fact, our next door neighbor's house was struck by lightning in one of those storms just a few years ago. Our house shook so hard, I thought it was an earthquake. Crazy!

What's your idea of fun?

Disneyland! I'm a huge Disney fan and love taking my family there. Both my husband and I grew up in Southern California, so it was a big part of our childhoods. He even worked at the Carnation Ice Cream Parlor on Main Street when he was sixteen.

What is your favorite song?

I love all kinds of music, but this book was inspired by my love for those old classic Southern spirituals. I guess my favorite is "This Little Light of Mine." It is a song about hope and love and faith in our ability to do great things.

Who is your favorite fictional character?

Kit from *The Witch of Blackbird Pond* by Elizabeth George Speare. She is sassy and smart and willing to stand up for what is right. I read that book in seventh grade and have loved and admired her ever since.

If you were stranded on a deserted island, who would you want for company?

My husband, because he's fairly resourceful and I bet he could make a radio from a coconut or a pair of roller skates from banana peels.

What is the best advice you have received about writing?

I went to an SCBWI (Society of Children's Book Writers and Illustrators) workshop in Los Angeles where Graham Salisbury, author of *Under the Blood Red Sun*, was speaking. He shared the idea of building word journals and said, "No one owns a word." That was powerful. I began following his suggestion to keep my own word journals, jotting down single words that struck me as interesting. Words like *plucked*, *howling*, *inky*, *swirl*. Then, when I feel stuck in my writing, I turn to my word journals for inspiration. It works wonders.

What advice do you wish someone had given you when you were younger?

Consider this question: What if you are greater than you suppose?

Do you ever get writer's block? What do you do to get back on track?

I don't think there is a writer out there who doesn't experience writer's block at some point. For me, it usually comes when I am putting too much pressure or expectation on my writing process. So, I step back. I take a nap and a walk and eat a tub of Ben and Jerry's Heath Bar Crunch ice cream. I think about other things. Then, when I'm ready to try writing again, I start by going through my word and picture journals. Pumping up my imagination and reconnecting with the fun side of writing gives me courage to face the blank page.

What do you want readers to remember about your books?

My characters become incredibly real to me. I would love it if readers felt the same way.

What would you do if you ever stopped writing?

Curl up and die.

What should people know about you?
I am allergic to mushrooms.

What do you like best about yourself?
My second toe is longer than my big toe. Only 18 percent of the population has this condition. In ancient Greece it was considered elite, and most statues reflect a longer second toe. In fact, the Statue of Liberty has the same toes I do!

Did you have any strange habits as a kid?
When I was young, I had a very specific way of loading the dishwasher. I had to separate the utensils because I was afraid that the knives would hurt the forks and the forks would hurt the spoons. They each had to be in their own compartment—for their own safety.

What do you consider to be your greatest accomplishment?
Without a doubt—being a mom to three amazing kiddos.

What do you wish you could do better?
Sing.

What would your readers be most surprised to learn about you?
My family narrowly escaped a carbon monoxide poisoning disaster when our boiler malfunctioned in October 2002. My oldest daughter (age eight at the time) woke me on a Sunday morning, saying she was sick. I also felt terrible and thought we all must have the flu. Something came to my mind and told me, very strongly, to go check on my two youngest children

(ages one and three). They were completely unresponsive. I grabbed them and hollered for my oldest to follow me out of the house. We called 911. The gas company told us that any carbon monoxide reading over 200 was considered lethal. The first reading they recorded as they walked into our home was 220. The reading in our basement was over 1,000! I keep the quarantine tag that they put on our home as a reminder that the universe has a purpose for my children. They could have easily been taken that day.

When twelve-year-old Jade
visits her aunt Elise in Wyoming, she
doesn't expect to get caught up in a Wild
West adventure. But when you become
friends with a boy who says he's
a descendant of Butch Cassidy,
do you have a choice?

Find out in Tess Hilmo's

Skies Like These

Jade should have let her expectations go when she first saw her aunt at the airport. She should have known there wouldn't be bearskin rugs and antlers hanging on the walls of Aunt Elise's house. She should have guessed she wouldn't be saddling up broncos or sliding turquoise rings on all of her fingers.

"Kitchen's in back," Aunt Elise said, disappearing down a narrow hallway. "I put some stew in the Crock-Pot this morning. You must be starving after that long flight."

Jade stepped past her luggage and followed her aunt. The hallway was dark, even though the sun was still shining bright outside, but she could make out a few pictures on the wall. One was of Aunt Elise at the summit of a mountain, possibly Grand Teton. Another showed two girls in plaid dresses and patent leather shoes standing on some steps. Jade leaned in and looked at those girls. She guessed the younger one to be her mother. Aunt Elise was the oldest by seven years, which would make her fifty-one.

"Come eat and then we'll check in with your folks," Aunt Elise called from the kitchen.

Jade started to go, but noticed a gilded frame at the end of the hallway. It was her baby picture. The one where she was swaddled in a white, crocheted blanket.

"You were an angel." Aunt Elise leaned against the kitchen doorjamb.

"Were you there?"

Aunt Elise came over to where Jade was standing. "Absolutely." She reached up and gently ran a finger along the frame. "I was there for all of your firsts—your first word, your first step, your first day of kindergarten."

Jade tried to remember her very first day at Washington Elementary. There was a tattered, wispy recollection of her aunt standing at her mother's side.

Aunt Elise clicked her tongue twice. "I would like to introduce you to someone." A silver bullet of fur streaked past Jade's legs and up into her aunt's arms. "This is Copernicus. The dogs rule the outside. Copernicus rules the inside."

"Copernicus," Jade said. "After the Renaissance astronomer."

"Do you know what the original Copernicus is most famous for?"

"Isn't he the one who first said the sun was at the center of our universe?"

"Correct!" Aunt Elise jabbed a finger in the air. "Everyone thought the earth was at the center of our planetary system. Copernicus challenged those assumptions, and do you know what they did?"

Jade didn't have a clue.

"They judged him harshly because they didn't understand him. They were afraid of his different views, called him crazy, and tried to lock him up." She shook her head. "Isn't that like people? To think we're the center of universe? Come, let's eat."

Aunt Elise handed the cat to Jade.

"Oh," Jade said, fumbling with the bundle of fur. "I don't really do cats."

Aunt Elise disappeared back into the kitchen. Copernicus pressed his head under Jade's chin, purring like a locomotive.

"Chow's ready," Aunt Elise called out.

Jade pulled Copernicus away from her chest and set him down on the orange, shag carpet. He eased between her feet, pressing his side against her ankles in a smooth, figure eight pattern. She stepped over him, careful not to trip, and into the kitchen.

Which was a sight to behold.

Paper stars bathed in silver glitter dangled from every inch of ceiling. Crammed in between the stars were Styrofoam balls painted in bright yellows, blues, and oranges.

"It's the solar system," Jade said, not able to take her eyes off the ceiling.

"It is. Roy made this for me. He snuck in one day while I was out and pinned all these up with fishing line. Pluto's represented as a planet and Saturn is off position, but it's pretty close. Can you imagine my surprise when I came home?"

"Who's Roy?"

Aunt Elise sat down at the round table and began eating her bowl of stew. "That," she said, "I'll let you discover for yourself."

Jade sat down across from her aunt, still mesmerized by the art hanging over her head. A small fan buzzed on the counter in the corner, offering enough breeze to send the paper stars twisting and turning. And, as they did, glints of glitter sent tiny shards of color and light shooting out across the room.

It was spectacular.

"Eat up," Aunt Elise said between bites. "I'm no Food Network Star, but it's hot and filling."

Jade's stomach rumbled. "I love watching the Food Network." She scooped a spoonful of potatoes and meat into her mouth. The moment her lips closed around the spoon, she knew there was a problem. It tasted awful and bits of slimy, chewy fat replaced what she thought was meat.

Aunt Elise looked up from her bowl and smiled.

Jade smiled back. "Mmmm," she said, forcing herself to swallow and ignore the gag reflex working into her throat.

"There's plenty more where that came from. I made enough to feed us for days."

"That's," Jade said slowly, "great."

Aunt Elise made a motion with her spoon, encouraging Jade to take a second bite.

Which she did. "I'm not very hungry," Jade said, forcing down the spoonful.

"Nonsense. You're like a chicken bone with a head. I'll fatten you up in no time."

The dogs out front began barking as the doorbell chimed.

"Excuse me." Aunt Elise left the kitchen for the front door.

Jade yanked her bowl off the table and placed it on the floor where Copernicus was stretched out, lazily thumping his tail against the sun drenched linoleum. He lifted his head, sniffed the stew and turned away. "So you agree," Jade said to the cat. She ran to the trash can in the corner and scooped the stew into an empty Cheerios box, being certain to close the lid and place a few crumpled napkins and wrappers on top. Then she put the empty bowl back on the table.

"Jade Landers, as I live and breathe. Coming to join us in the paradise of Wyoming."

Jade looked up to see a boy with a round, freckled face standing at the back door. He was in full cowboy gear—a wide brimmed hat, pointy cowboy boots, worn out Wranglers and an overgrown, silver belt buckle. "Do I know you?"

"LeRoy Parker. After *the* Leroy Parker." He yanked off his hat and turned his head sideways, offering up a profile.

"And that is . . . ?"

A flash of shock passed across his eyes. "Leroy Parker?" He was clearly distressed. "Better known as Butch Cassidy? Surely you people in Philadelphia have heard of Butch Cassidy!"

"How old are you?"

"Twelve, just like Elise told me you are."

Jade thought he looked short for twelve. "She's at the front door."

"I know. I rang the bell because I wanted to meet you on my own."

Understanding lit into Jade's mind. "Oh, *LeRoy*. You must be the Roy who made all of this." She waved her hands up toward the dazzling ceiling art.

A smile pulled across Roy's face. "Like it?"

"It's not bad."

Roy tilted his head to the Crock-Pot full of bubbling stew. "You didn't eat that, did you?"

"Pure poison."

"Hungry?"

"Famished."

Roy tugged his hat back on. Then he pulled out a Butterfinger candy bar, stripped off the wrapper and snapped it in half. "If there's one thing I've learned from my great, great uncle Butch Cassidy, it's that a real cowboy should always help a damsel in distress." He lined up the halves of candy bar side by side and handed Jade the larger of the two. "Welcome to Wyoming," he said, warm as the day. "You've come just in time."

"That's strange," Aunt Elise said, coming back into the kitchen. Then she saw Roy. "Have you been up to your tricks again?"

Jade shoved the last of the Butterfinger into her

mouth. "Roy was saying I came just in time."

"Just in time for what?" Aunt Elise asked.

"That's what I was wondering."

Roy glared at Jade and turned a smile on Aunt Elise. "Oh," he said, "you know."

Both Aunt Elise and Jade looked blankly at Roy.

"Just in time," he continued, stuttering and stumbling over his words, "to see the Wilson's heifer calve. She's about to pop any day now."

"Gee. Glad I won't miss that," Jade said, dripping sarcasm.

Roy gave her the stink eye and mouthed something that looked like *later*.

"Well, you be sure to come tell us when their cow goes into labor," Aunt Elise said. "A person should see something like that at least once in their life. Wouldn't you agree, Jade?"

"At least once."

Aunt Elise stirred the stew in the Crock-Pot. "You want some chow, Roy?"

"Nah." He was tucking his already tucked shirt into his jeans, clearly trying to show off his belt buckle. "I've got official business to attend to."

"Will we see you for stars tonight?"

"I wouldn't miss it!"

"What are stars?" Jade asked.

"You don't know what stars are?" Roy laughed. "You're more city than I thought."

Aunt Elise put a lid on the stew. "I think she was talking about the event more than the objects." She turned to Jade. "I have an observation deck on my roof."

"Nine thirty?" Roy asked.

"Sharp," Aunt Elise said. "Bring your parents; we'll make it a party." She gestured up to the paper stars and Styrofoam planets that filled her ceiling and said to Jade, "If you think this is beautiful, you'll love the real thing. A night sky is the best Wyoming has to offer. Remember how you were asking me how I knew you'd love it here? Come up on my roof and see the stars, then you'll understand."